THE USBORNE PICTURE DICTIONARY IN SPANISH

Felicity Brooks and Mairi Mackinnon
Designer and modelmaker: Jo Litchfield

Spanish language consultants: Pilar Dunster and Marta Núñez

Design and additional illustrations by
Mike Olley and Brian Voakes

Photography by Howard Allman

Contents

How to say the words

You can hear all the Spanish words in this book, read by a Spanish-speaking person, on the Usborne Quicklinks Web site at **www.usborne-quicklinks.com** All you need is an Internet connection and a computer that can play sounds. Find out more on page 112.

Using your dictionary

You can use this dictionary to find out how to say things in Spanish. Each page has 12 main words in English, with the same words in Spanish (the translations).

The English words are in the order of the alphabet: words beginning with A are first in the book. There are also pictures to show what words mean.

This letter in a blue square shows the first letter of the English words on that page.

This word shows the first English word on the page.

This word shows the last English word on the page.

All the English words are shown in blue. The Spanish translations are shown in black.

Don't forget that in a dictionary you read down the page in columns. In most other books you read across.

Short sentences or phrases, in English and in Spanish, show you how the word can be used.

If you forget the order of the letters in the alphabet, look at the bottom of any page.

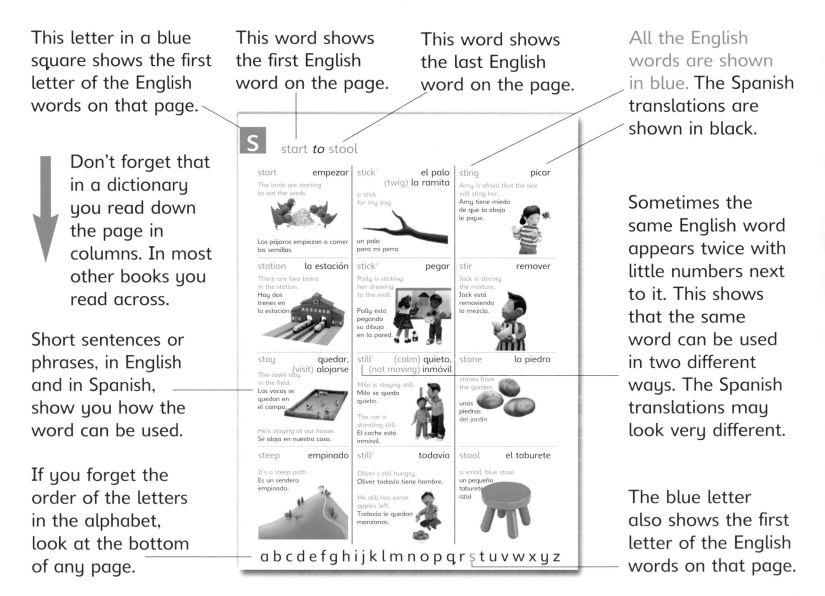

S start *to* stool

| start | empezar |
| The birds are starting to eat the seeds. |
| Los pájaros empiezan a comer las semillas. |

| stick¹ | el palo |
| | (twig) la ramita |
| a stick for my dog |
| un palo para mi perro |

| sting | picar |
| Amy is afraid that the bee will sting her. |
| Amy tiene miedo de que la abeja le pique. |

| station | la estación |
| There are two trains in the station. |
| Hay dos trenes en la estación. |

| stick² | pegar |
| Polly is sticking her drawing to the wall. |
| Polly está pegando su dibujo en la pared. |

| stir | remover |
| Jack is stirring the mixture. |
| Jack está removiendo la mezcla. |

| stay | quedar, (visit) alojarse |
| The cows stay in the field. |
| Las vacas se quedan en el campo. |
| He's staying at our house. |
| Se aloja en nuestra casa. |

| still¹ | (calm) quieto, (not moving) inmóvil |
| Milo is staying still. |
| Milo se queda quieto. |
| The car is standing still. |
| El coche está inmóvil. |

| stone | la piedra |
| stones from the garden. |
| unas piedras del jardín |

| steep | empinado |
| It's a steep path. |
| Es un sendero empinado. |

| still² | todavía |
| Oliver's still hungry. |
| Oliver todavía tiene hambre. |
| He still has some apples left. |
| Todavía le quedan manzanas. |

| stool | el taburete |
| a small, blue stool |
| un pequeño taburete azul |

a b c d e f g h i j k l m n o p q r s t u v w x y z

Sometimes the same English word appears twice with little numbers next to it. This shows that the same word can be used in two different ways. The Spanish translations may look very different.

The blue letter also shows the first letter of the English words on that page.

How to find a word

1 Think of the letter the word starts with. "Stone" starts with an "s", for example.

2 Look through the dictionary until you have found the "s" pages.

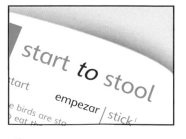

3 Think of the next letter of the word. Look for words that begin with "st".

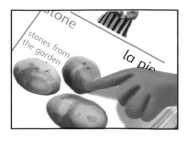

4 Now look down all the "st" words until you find your word.

El or la?

In Spanish, all nouns, or "naming" words such as "boy" and "house", are either masculine or feminine. The Spanish word for "the" is *el* for masculine nouns, and *la* for feminine nouns.

Sometimes you can guess whether a noun is masculine or feminine – for example, "boy" is masculine (*el chico*). Almost all nouns ending in *–o* are masculine, and almost all nouns ending in *–a* are feminine. For other words, you need to check in the dictionary.*

Masculine or feminine?

Which of these fruits are masculine, and which are feminine?

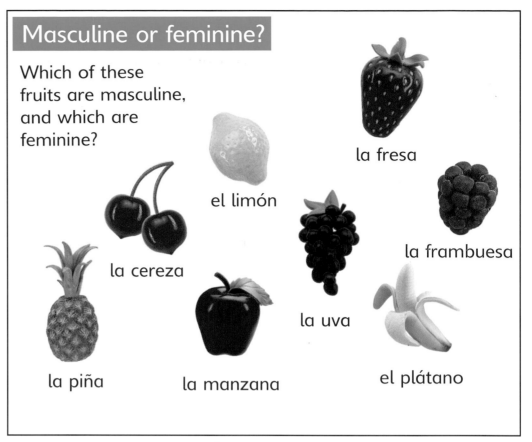

el limón

la fresa

la cereza

la frambuesa

la uva

la piña

la manzana

el plátano

Answers: limón and plátano are masculine.
Cereza, frambuesa, fresa, manzana and piña are feminine.

Looking at a word

When you look up a word, here are some of the things you can find out.

You can check how to spell the word in English.

You can see how you might use the word in English and in Spanish.

These words in brackets show that you can use the word in different ways.

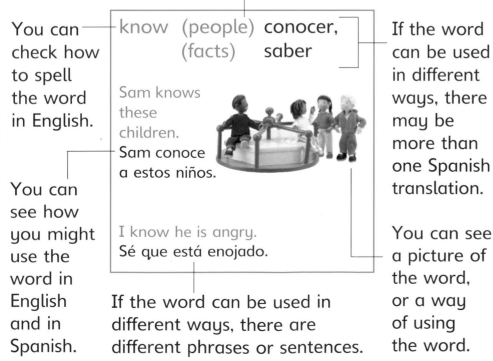

know (people) conocer,
(facts) saber

Sam knows these children.
Sam conoce a estos niños.

I know he is angry.
Sé que está enojado.

If the word can be used in different ways, there are different phrases or sentences.

If the word can be used in different ways, there may be more than one Spanish translation.

You can see a picture of the word, or a way of using the word.

Plurals

"Plural" means "more than one". The Spanish for "the" when you are talking about more than one is *los* for masculine nouns, or masculine and feminine together, and *las* for feminine nouns. You also add *s* to the end of the noun if it ends in *a*, *e* or *o*, and *es* if it ends in any other letter**:

child	el niño *or* la niña
children	los niños
house	la casa
houses	las casas
clock	el reloj
clocks	los relojes
town	la ciudad
towns	las ciudades

*A very few words that begin with "a" are feminine but use *el*. They are shown in the dictionary like this: water   el agua (f)

** Nouns ending in *–z* change to *–ces*, for example fish   el pez   los peces

Adjectives

"Describing" words, such as "small" or "expensive", are called adjectives. In Spanish, they almost always go after the noun they are describing. The endings may change, depending whether the noun is masculine or feminine, singular or plural. For example, the Spanish for "new" is *nuevo*:

the new car
> el coche nuevo

For a feminine noun, you change the –o at the end to –a:

the new house
> la casa nueva

If the adjective ends in –e, the ending doesn't change:

the big car
> el coche grande

the big house
> la casa grande

For plurals, you add –s to the end of the adjective:

the new cars
> los coches nuevos

the new houses
> las casas nuevas

the big cars
> los coches grandes

the big houses
> las casas grandes

If an adjective ends in any letter except a, e or o, it is the same for both masculine and feminine. For plurals, you add –es:

the blue house
> la casa azul

the blue cars
> los coches azules

Verbs

"Doing" words, such as "walk" or "laugh" are called verbs. In English, verbs don't change very much, whoever is doing them:

I walk, you walk, he walks

In Spanish, the endings change much more. Many verbs work in a similar way to the one below. This verb is in the present – the form that you use to talk about what is happening now. You don't usually need to say "I", "you" and so on, as you can mostly tell from the verb itself who is doing it.

to talk	hablar
I talk	hablo
you talk*	hablas
you talk*	(usted) habla
he talks	habla
she talks	habla
we talk	hablamos
you talk*	(ustedes) hablan
they talk	hablan

In the main part of the dictionary, you will find the "to" form of the verb. On pages 100-104 at the back of the book, you will find a list of all the verbs, with the most useful forms in the present: the "to" form, the "–ing" form, the "I" form and the "he" or "she" form.

The verbs for "to be"

One of the most useful verbs to know is "to be". In Spanish, there are actually two verbs: *ser* and *estar*.

to be	ser
I am	soy
you are*	eres
you are*	(usted) es
he is	es
she is	es
we are	somos
you are*	(ustedes) son
they are	son

to be	estar
I am	estoy
you are*	estás
you are*	(usted) está
he is	está
she is	está
we are	estamos
you are	(ustedes) están
they are	están

You use "ser" for things that don't change:

La casa es grande.
> The house is large.

Papá es mayor.
> Dad is a grown-up.

You use "estar" for things that can change:

Estoy cansado.
> I am tired.

La tienda está cerrada.
> The store is closed.

* In Spanish, you use the –as form for one person, either a young person or someone you know very well. For someone you don't know very well, you use the –a form with *usted* (a special polite word for "you"). You use the *(ustedes)* –an form for more than one person.

4

Aa

actor   el actor
la actriz

The actors are waving.
Los actores
saludan.

(to be) afraid   tener miedo

Maddy
is afraid
of spiders.
Maddy tiene
miedo a las arañas.

air   el aire

The red balloon
is floating in
the air.
El globo rojo
flota en el aire.

add   añadir

Billy's adding some
blocks to his tower.
Billy añade unos
cubos a su torre.

after   después

Sacha goes
after Suki.
Sacha baja
después de
Suki.

Sacha

Suki

alone   solo

Katie sings when she's alone.
Katie canta cuando está sola.

address   la dirección

This is Oliver's address.
Ésta es la dirección de Oliver.

Oliver Comelotodo
C/ Desayuno 4, 3°
51000 Merienda

afternoon   la tarde

three o'clock in the afternoon
las tres de la tarde

alphabet   el alfabeto

*abcdefghijklm
nopqrstuvwxyz*

the letters of the alphabet
las letras del alfabeto

adult   el adulto
la adulta

Minnie is a
child. Her dad
is an adult.
Minnie es una
niña. Su papá
es un adulto.

age   la edad

What age
is Olivia?

Ben

Joshua

Olivia

¿Qué edad tiene Olivia?

ambulance   la ambulancia

There is nobody in the
ambulance.

No hay
nadie en la
ambulancia.

a b c d e f g h i j k l m n o p q r s t u v w x y z

amount — **la cantidad**

a large amount of pasta
una gran cantidad de pasta

ankle — **el tobillo**

Ankles join legs to feet.

Los tobillos unen las piernas con los pies.

apple — **la manzana**

Apples are very healthy fruit.
Las manzanas son una fruta muy sana.

angel — **el ángel**

a Christmas angel

un ángel de Navidad

answer — **la respuesta**

Question: Which animal says meow?
Answer: A cat.
Pregunta: ¿Qué animal hace miau?
Respuesta: El gato.

arm — **el brazo**

This is Jack's left arm.
Éste es el brazo izquierdo de Jack.

angry — **enojado**

Jack is angry with Pip.
Jack está enojado con Pip.

ant — **la hormiga**

The ants are looking for something to eat.
Las hormigas están buscando algo que comer.

arrive — **llegar**

The bus arrives at one o'clock.
El autobús llega a la una.

animal — **el animal**

A lion is an animal.

El león es un animal.

ape — **el mono**

An orangutan is a kind of ape.

El orangután es un tipo de mono.

art — **el arte**

It's a work of art.
Es una obra de arte.

a b c d e f g h i j k l m n o p q r s t u v w x y z

artist   el artista / la artista

The artist is painting some flowers.
La artista está pintando unas flores.

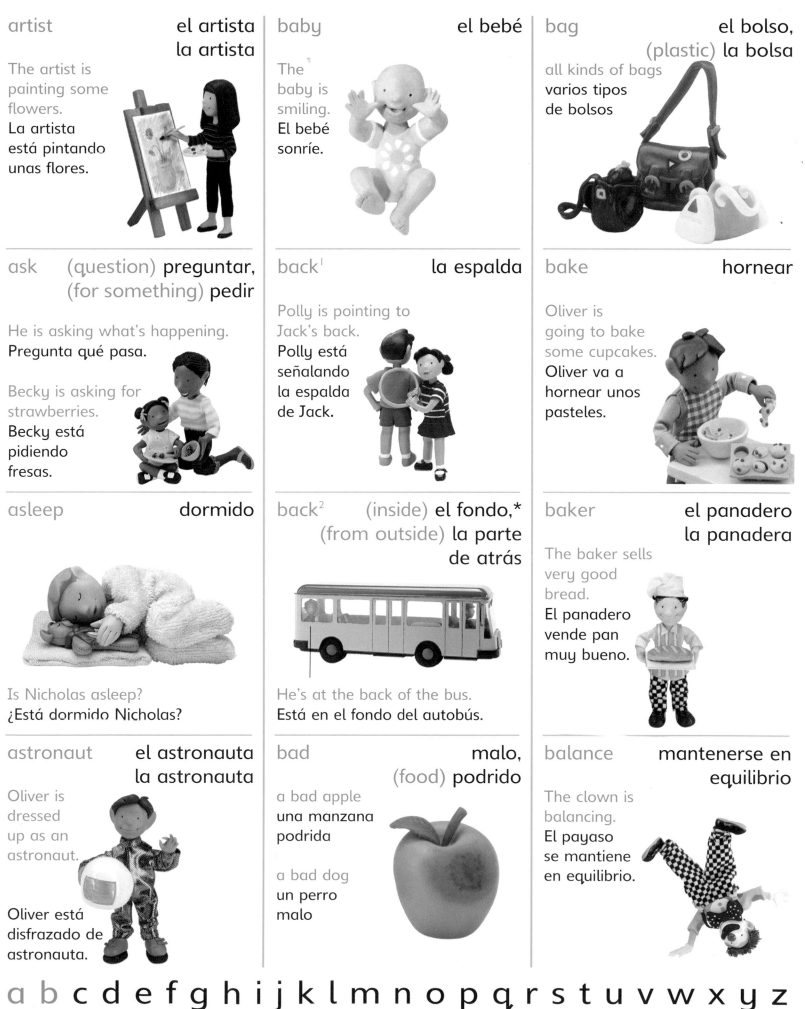

ask   (question) preguntar, (for something) pedir

He is asking what's happening.
Pregunta qué pasa.

Becky is asking for strawberries.
Becky está pidiendo fresas.

asleep   dormido

Is Nicholas asleep?
¿Está dormido Nicholas?

astronaut   el astronauta / la astronauta

Oliver is dressed up as an astronaut.
Oliver está disfrazado de astronauta.

baby   el bebé

The baby is smiling.
El bebé sonríe.

back¹   la espalda

Polly is pointing to Jack's back.
Polly está señalando la espalda de Jack.

back²   (inside) el fondo,* (from outside) la parte de atrás

He's at the back of the bus.
Está en el fondo del autobús.

bad   malo, (food) podrido

a bad apple
una manzana podrida

a bad dog
un perro malo

bag   el bolso, (plastic) la bolsa

all kinds of bags
varios tipos de bolsos

bake   hornear

Oliver is going to bake some cupcakes.
Oliver va a hornear unos pasteles.

baker   el panadero / la panadera

The baker sells very good bread.
El panadero vende pan muy bueno.

balance   mantenerse en equilibrio

The clown is balancing.
El payaso se mantiene en equilibrio.

a b c d e f g h i j k l m n o p q r s t u v w x y z

* Spanish uses the same word, *el fondo*, for the back or bottom of: a room, a bus, a cup or glass, a lake, the sea. The outside is different: the bus has a poster on the back. El autobús lleva un anuncio en la parte de atrás.

bald — **calvo**

Mr. Rogers is bald.
El señor Rogers es calvo.

banana — **el plátano**

A banana is a yellow fruit.
El plátano es una fruta amarilla.

bar — **la barra**

a steel bar
una barra de acero

Hold on to the bar!
¡Agárrate bien a la barra!

ball — **la pelota**

a brightly colored ball
una pelota de colores fuertes

band — **la orquesta**

Polly and Marco play in a band.
Polly y Marco tocan en una orquesta.

bare — **desnudo**

Marcus is bare for his bath.
Marcus está desnudo porque se va a bañar.

ballerina — **la bailarina**

Lucy is a ballerina.
Lucy es bailarina.

bang — **pum**

Bang! The balloon bursts.

¡¡Pum!!

¡Pum! El globo explota.

bark[1] — **la corteza**

the bark of a tree
la corteza de un árbol

balloon — **el globo**

a pink balloon
un globo rosa

a balloon ride
un viaje en globo

bank — **el banco**

Mr. Brand is getting money from the bank.
El señor Brand saca dinero del banco.

bark[2] — **ladrar**

Pip is barking.
Pip está ladrando.

¡Guau Guau!

a b c d e f g h i j k l m n o p q r s t u v w x y z

barn   **el granero**

The barn is full of hay.
El granero está lleno de heno.

bathtub   **la bañera**

The bathtub is empty.
La bañera está vacía.

bear   **el oso**

A bear is a wild animal.
El oso es un animal salvaje.

base   **la base**

The lamp has a yellow base.
La lámpara tiene una base amarilla.

beach   **la playa**

They are playing on the beach.

Están jugando en la playa.

beard   **la barba**

Mr. Brown has a beard.
El señor Brown tiene barba.

basket   **el cesto**

a big, round basket
un gran cesto redondo

beak   **el pico**

A toucan has a big beak.
El tucán tiene un pico grande.

beautiful   **hermoso**

a beautiful pink cake
un hermoso pastel rosa

bat (animal) **el murciélago,** (for sports) **el bate, la paleta**

A bat isn't a bird.

El murciélago no es un pájaro.

a baseball bat
un bate de béisbol

bean   **la habichuela**

green beans   las habichuelas verdes

bed   **la cama**

a child's bed
una cama de niño

a b c d e f g h i j k l m n o p q r s t u v w x y z

bedroom   el dormitorio

Ben's bedroom   el dormitorio de Ben

bee   la abeja

Bees make honey.
Las abejas hacen la miel.

beetle   el escarabajo

Beetles have six legs.
Los escarabajos tienen seis patas.

beetroot   la remolacha

Beetroot grows underground.
La remolacha crece bajo tierra.

before   antes

Suki goes before Sacha.
Suki baja antes de Sacha.

Sacha

Suki

begin   empezar

Sam's beginning to fall asleep.
Sam empieza a dormirse.

behind   detrás

The kitten is behind the flowerpot.
El gatito está detrás de la maceta.

belong   pertenecer

The book belongs to Suzie.
El libro pertenece a Suzie.

below   debajo

The kitten is below the boards.

El gatito está debajo de las tablas.

belt   el cinturón

a brown leather belt
un cinturón marrón de cuero

beside   al lado

The kitten is beside the flowerpot.
El gatito está al lado de la maceta.

between   entre

The kitten is between the two flowerpots.

El gatito está entre las dos macetas.

a b c d e f g h i j k l m n o p q r s t u v w x y z

bib *to* book

bib   **el babero**

a baby's bib
un babero de bebé

bicycle   **la bicicleta**

Sara's blue bicycle
la bicicleta azul de Sara

big   **gran, grande**

a very big animal
un animal muy grande

bird   **el pájaro**

Not all birds can fly.
No todos los pájaros vuelan.

birthday   **el cumpleaños**

a birthday party
una fiesta de cumpleaños

bite   **morder**

Jon is biting an apple.
Jon está mordiendo una manzana.

blanket   **la manta**

a wool blanket
una manta de lana

blow   **soplar, (blow out) apagar**

Polly is blowing out the candles.
Polly apaga las velas.

boat   **el bote**

a rowboat
un bote de remos

body   **el cuerpo**

some parts of the body
algunas partes del cuerpo

arm el brazo

tummy el estómago

leg la pierna

foot el pie

bone   **el hueso**

Patch has found some bones.
Patch ha encontrado unos huesos.

book   **el libro**

Tina is reading a book.
Tina está leyendo un libro.

a b c d e f g h i j k l m n o p q r s t u v w x y z

b

boot *to* breakfast

boot — la bota

Alex wears boots when it's raining.

Alex lleva botas cuando llueve.

bottle — la botella

glass and plastic bottles
unas botellas de vidrio y de plástico

bottom¹ — el trasero

Jack's bottom is in the circle.

El trasero de Jack está en el círculo.

bottom² (cup, sea) **el fondo,** (hill, stairs) **el pie**

The kitten is at the bottom of the stairs.

El gatito está al pie de la escalera.

bowl — el bol

a plastic bowl
un bol de plástico

box — la caja

a cardboard box
una caja de cartón

boy — el chico

Oliver and Robert are boys.

Oliver y Robert son chicos.

branch — la rama

two birds on a branch

dos pájaros en una rama

brave — valiente

Mr. Sparks is very brave. El señor Sparks es muy valiente.

bread — el pan

a loaf of bread
un pan

break — romper

Asha has broken the vase.
Asha ha roto el florero.

breakfast — el desayuno

a healthy breakfast
un desayuno sano

a b c d e f g h i j k l m n o p q r s t u v w x y z

12

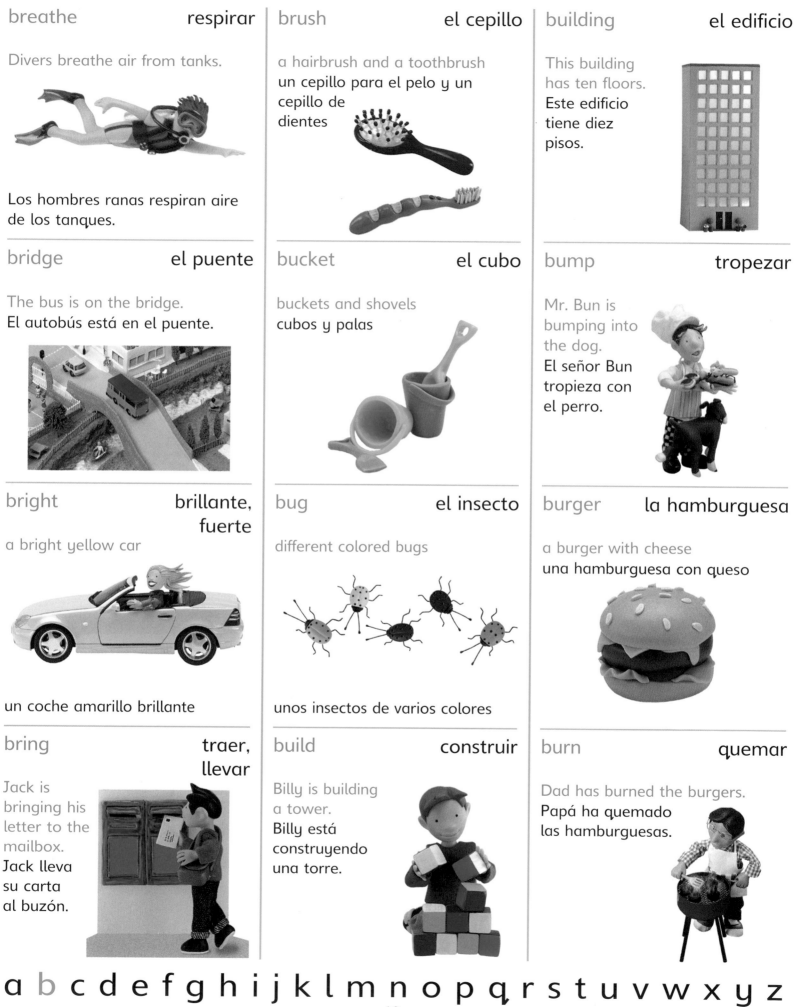

breathe — respirar

Divers breathe air from tanks.

Los hombres ranas respiran aire de los tanques.

bridge — el puente

The bus is on the bridge.
El autobús está en el puente.

bright — brillante, fuerte

a bright yellow car

un coche amarillo brillante

bring — traer, llevar

Jack is bringing his letter to the mailbox.
Jack lleva su carta al buzón.

brush — el cepillo

a hairbrush and a toothbrush
un cepillo para el pelo y un cepillo de dientes

bucket — el cubo

buckets and shovels
cubos y palas

bug — el insecto

different colored bugs

unos insectos de varios colores

build — construir

Billy is building a tower.
Billy está construyendo una torre.

building — el edificio

This building has ten floors.
Este edificio tiene diez pisos.

bump — tropezar

Mr. Bun is bumping into the dog.
El señor Bun tropieza con el perro.

burger — la hamburguesa

a burger with cheese
una hamburguesa con queso

burn — quemar

Dad has burned the burgers.
Papá ha quemado las hamburguesas.

a b c d e f g h i j k l m n o p q r s t u v w x y z

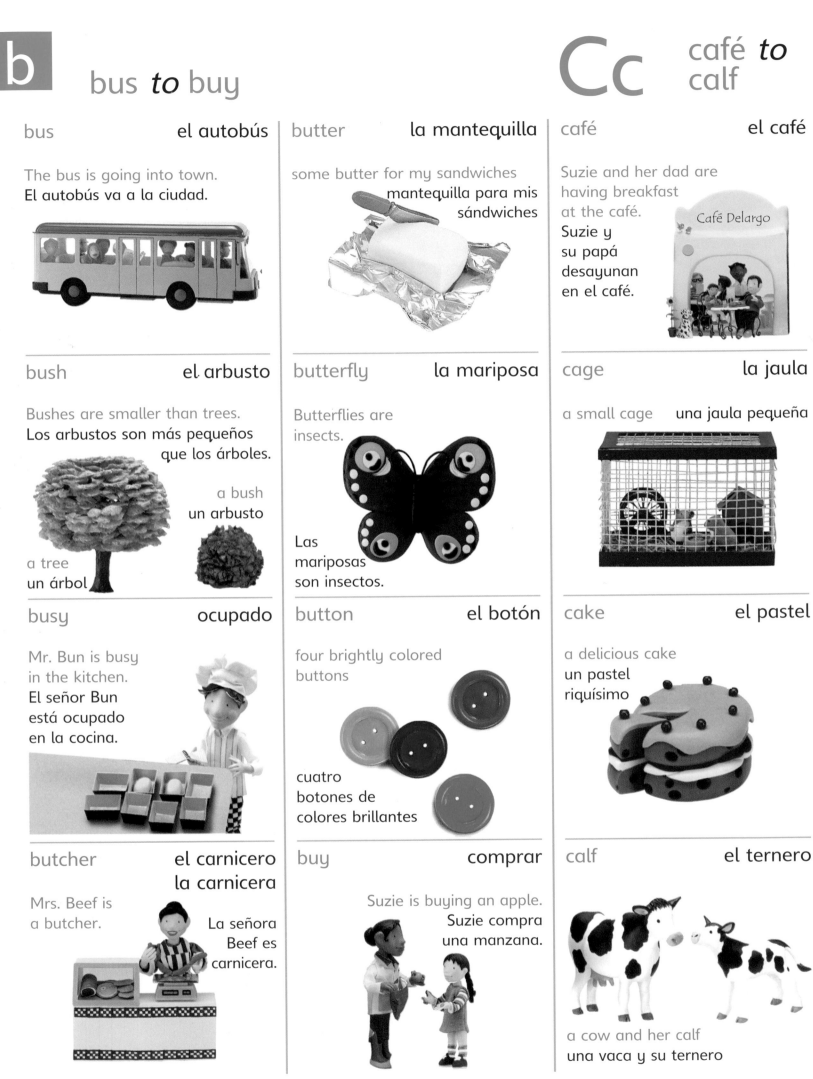

bus   el autobús

The bus is going into town.
El autobús va a la ciudad.

butter   la mantequilla

some butter for my sandwiches
mantequilla para mis sándwiches

café   el café

Suzie and her dad are having breakfast at the café.
Suzie y su papá desayunan en el café.

Café Delargo

bush   el arbusto

Bushes are smaller than trees.
Los arbustos son más pequeños que los árboles.

a bush
un arbusto

a tree
un árbol

butterfly   la mariposa

Butterflies are insects.

Las mariposas son insectos.

cage   la jaula

a small cage   una jaula pequeña

busy   ocupado

Mr. Bun is busy in the kitchen.
El señor Bun está ocupado en la cocina.

button   el botón

four brightly colored buttons

cuatro botones de colores brillantes

cake   el pastel

a delicious cake
un pastel riquísimo

butcher   el carnicero
la carnicera

Mrs. Beef is a butcher.

La señora Beef es carnicera.

buy   comprar

Suzie is buying an apple.
Suzie compra una manzana.

calf   el ternero

a cow and her calf
una vaca y su ternero

a b c d e f g h i j k l m n o p q r s t u v w x y z

call *to* castle

call — **llamar**

Alex is calling Pip.
Alex llama a Pip.

¡Ven, Pip!

Polly calls her doll "Celestine".
Polly llama "Celestine" a su muñeca.

candle — **la vela**

a cake with eight candles
un pastel con ocho velas

carpet — **la alfombra**

a room with blue carpet

una habitación con alfombra azul

camel — **el camello**

A camel can have one or two humps.

Un camello puede tener una o dos gibas.

cap — **la gorra**

a baseball cap
una gorra de béisbol

carrot — **la zanahoria**

Carrots are vegetables.

Las zanahorias son verduras.

camera — **la cámara**

This camera is easy to use.
Esta cámara es fácil de utilizar.

car — **el coche**

a sports car
un coche deportivo

carry — **llevar**

Aggie is carrying some flowers.
Aggie lleva unas flores.

camp — **acampar, ir de camping**

They are camping.
Van de camping.

card — **la tarjeta**

I have three birthday cards.
Tengo tres tarjetas de cumpleaños.

castle — **el castillo**

an old castle **un castillo antiguo**

a b c d e f g h i j k l m n o p q r s t u v w x y z

15

cat   **el gato**

The cat is licking its paw.
El gato se lame la pata.

cave   **la cueva**

There's a bear in the cave.
Hay un oso en la cueva.

chair   **la silla**

a small, blue chair
una pequeña silla azul

catch   **agarrar**

Jack is catching the ball.
Jack agarra la pelota.

CD   **el CD**

my favorite CD
mi CD preferido

chalk   **la tiza**

a chalk drawing
un dibujo hecho con tiza

caterpillar   **la oruga**

two caterpillars dancing

dos orugas que bailan

center   **el centro**

The fruit is in the center of the table.

La fruta está en el centro de la mesa.

chase   **perseguir**

Polly and Jack are chasing the dogs.
Polly y Jack persiguen a los perros.

cauliflower   **la coliflor**

A cauliflower is a vegetable.
La coliflor es una verdura.

cereal   **los cereales**

I eat cereal for my breakfast.
Como cereales para desayunar.

cheap   **barato**

Everything is cheap in this store.
Todo es barato en esta tienda.

a b c d e f g h i j k l m n o p q r s t u v w x y z

cheese — el queso

Swiss cheese
queso suizo

chicken — el pollo

I like roast chicken.

Me gusta
el pollo asado.

choose — elegir

Billy is choosing
between the
apple and
the cupcake.
Billy elige
entre la
manzana
y el pastel.

chef — el cocinero
la cocinera

Mr. Cook is a chef.
El señor
Cook es
cocinero.

child — el niño
la niña

three children
tres niños

city — la ciudad

There are a lot of
buildings in a city.
Hay muchos edificios
en una ciudad.

cherry — la cereza

Cherries are red fruit.
Las cerezas son unas
frutas rojas.

chin — la barbilla

Jack's chin — la barbilla de Jack

class — la clase

Mr. Levy's class
la clase del
señor Levy

chick — el pollito

This hen has
five chicks.

Esta gallina tiene cinco pollitos.

chocolate — el chocolate

a bar of chocolate
una tableta
de chocolate

classroom — el aula (f)

our classroom — nuestra aula

a b c d e f g h i j k l m n o p q r s t u v w x y z

clean¹   **limpiar**

Please clean the glass!

¡Limpia la ventana por favor!

clean²   **limpio**

Only Neil has clean clothes.
Sólo Neil tiene la ropa limpia.

climb   **subir**

Mr. Sparks is climbing the ladder to rescue the cat.
El señor Sparks sube la escalera para rescatar al gato.

clock   **el reloj**

That clock is very noisy.
Ese reloj hace mucho ruido.

close¹   **cerrar**

Danny is closing the door.
Danny cierra la puerta.

close²   **cerca**

Bill is close to Ben.
Bill está cerca de Ben.

clothes   **la ropa**

clean clothes

ropa limpia

cloud   **la nube**

a big, white cloud
una gran nube blanca

clown   **el payaso**

Look, the clown is juggling.

Mira, el payaso hace malabarismos.

coat   **el abrigo**

Renata is wearing a red coat.
Renata lleva un abrigo rojo.

coffee   **el café**

Coffee has a strong taste.
El café tiene un gusto fuerte.

coin   **la moneda**

Pete has two coins in his hand.
Pete tiene dos monedas en la mano.

a b c d e f g h i j k l m n o p q r s t u v w x y z

cold¹   el resfrío

Helen has a bad cold.
Helen tiene un fuerte resfrío.

cold²   frío

Ash wears gloves when it's cold.

Ash lleva guantes cuando hace frío.

color   el color

bright colors   colores brillantes

green
verde

red
rojo

blue
azul

yellow
amarillo

comb   el peine

a plastic comb
un peine de plástico

come   venir, llegar

The clown is coming to my party.
El payaso viene a mi fiesta.

The bus comes at one o'clock.
El autobús llega a la una.

computer   la computadora

I work on a computer.
Trabajo con una computadora.

cook   hacer, cocinar

Dad is cooking pancakes.
Papá hace unas tortitas.

copy   copiar

Sally's copying what Polly's doing.
Sally copia lo que hace Polly.

country¹   el país

The map shows the countries of Africa.
El mapa muestra los países de África.

country²   el campo

springtime in the country

la primavera en el campo

cow   la vaca

Cows give milk.
Las vacas dan leche.

crash   estrellarse

The car has crashed into the tree.
El coche se ha estrellado contra un árbol.

a b c d e f g h i j k l m n o p q r s t u v w x y z

crawl · **gatear**

This baby is crawling.

Este bebé gatea.

crayon · **el lápiz de cera**

a box of crayons
una caja de lápices de cera

creep · **ir de puntillas**

Anna is creeping into the kitchen.

Anna va de puntillas a la cocina.

crocodile · **el cocodrilo**

Crocodiles live near water.
Los cocodrilos viven cerca del agua.

cross[1] · **la cruz**

A cross is made of two lines.

Una cruz está hecha de dos rayas.

cross[2] · **cruzar**

a good place
to cross
the street

un buen sitio para cruzar la calle

crown · **la corona**

Kings and queens wear crowns.
Los reyes llevan coronas.

cry · **llorar**

Ross is crying because he has a stomach ache.

Ross llora porque le duele el estómago.

cucumber · **el pepino**

slices of cucumber

unas rodajas de pepino

cup · **la taza**

I have my tea in a green cup.
Tomo mi té en una taza verde.

cut · **cortar, (cut out) recortar**

Danny is cutting a circle.

Danny recorta un círculo.

cycle · **ir en bicicleta**

Sara cycles to school.
Sara va a la escuela en bicicleta.

a b c d e f g h i j k l m n o p q r s t u v w x y z

dance   bailar

Stef and Laura are dancing.
Stef y Laura están bailando.

dangerous   peligroso

a dangerous snake
una serpiente peligrosa

dark   (color) oscuro, (not daylight) de noche

It's dark already.
Ya es de noche.

dark blue
azul oscuro

date   la fecha

What's the date on the calendar?

Enero

Lunes	Martes	Miércoles	Jueves	Viernes	Sábado	Domingo
		1	2	3	4	5
6	7	8	9	10	11	12
13	14	15	16	17	18	19
20	21	22	23	24	25	26
27	28	29	30	31		

¿Qué fecha marca el calendario?

day   el día

The sun shines all day.

El sol brilla todo el día.

dear   querido

Querido Javi :
Muchas grac
regalo preci
Me gusta

Querida Ana :
Muchas gracias por la invitación a tu fiesta de cumpleaños el 26 de mayo.
Me encantaría ir.

deep   profundo

a deep hole
un hoyo profundo

deer   el ciervo

Deer live on hills and in woods.
Los ciervos viven en los montes y en los bosques.

delicious   riquísimo

Jack's sandwich is delicious.
El sándwich de Jack es riquísimo.

dentist   el dentista / la dentista

I'm not afraid of the dentist.
No tengo miedo del dentista.

desert   el desierto

Very few plants grow in the desert.
Poquísimas plantas crecen en el desierto.

desk   el escritorio

My desk has six drawers.
Mi escritorio tiene seis cajones.

a b c **d** e f g h i j k l m n o p q r s t u v w x y z

dictionary   el diccionario

A dictionary can explain what
words mean.
Un diccionario
puede explicar
lo que quieren
decir las
palabras.

USBORNE
**PICTURE
DICTIONARY**

dig   cavar

Anna is
digging a hole.
Anna cava
un hoyo.

dirty   sucio

Sally's
clothes are
very dirty.

La ropa de
Sally está
muy sucia.

die   morirse

My plant is dying because
of the heat.
Mi planta se
está muriendo
por el calor.

digger   la excavadora

a big, yellow digger

una gran
excavadora
amarilla

disappear   desaparecer

Polly's dog has
disappeared.

El perro de
Polly ha
desaparecido.

different   diferente

The twins wear different colors.

Las gemelas llevan colores
diferentes.

dinner   la cena

It's time for
dinner.
Es la hora
de la cena.

dive   tirarse al agua

Jack is diving into the pool.
Jack se tira al agua
en la piscina.

difficult   difícil

It's difficult to take
care of two babies
at the same time.
Es difícil cuidar
a dos bebés a
la vez.

dinosaur   el dinosaurio

an enormous dinosaur
un dinosaurio enorme

diver   el hombre rana

The diver is looking for coral.
El hombre rana está buscando
coral.

a b c d e f g h i j k l m n o p q r s t u v w x y z

do   **hacer**

Jenny is doing a
jigsaw puzzle.
**Jenny está haciendo
un rompecabezas.**

I'm doing my
homework.
**Estoy haciendo
mis deberes.**

doctor   **el médico, la médica**

The doctor is taking care of Kirsty.
**El médico está cuidando
a Kirsty.**

dog   **el perro**

a nice dog   **un perro simpático**

doll   **la muñeca**

What's your
doll's name?

**¿Cómo se
llama tu
muñeca?**

dolphin   **el delfín**

A dolphin isn't a fish.

**El delfín no
es un pez.**

donkey   **el burro**

A donkey looks like
a small horse.
**Un burro
se parece
a un
caballo
pequeño.**

door   **la puerta**

The front door is red.
La puerta de entrada es roja.

down   **hacia abajo**

This arrow
points down.
**Esta flecha
apunta hacia
abajo.**

dragon   **el dragón**

A dragon is a kind of monster.
**Un dragón es una especie
de monstruo.**

draw   **dibujar**

Molly is drawing a face.

**Molly dibuja
una cara.**

drawing   **el dibujo**

Molly's
drawing
**el dibujo
de Molly**

dream   **el sueño**

Adam is having
a strange
dream.

**Adam tiene
un sueño extraño.**

a b c d e f g h i j k l m n o p q r s t u v w x y z

dress¹　　el vestido

Anya is wearing a red dress with white flowers.
Anya lleva un vestido rojo con flores blancas.

dress²　　vestirse

Robert is dressing himself.
Robert se viste.

drink　　beber

Polly is drinking orange juice.
Polly está bebiendo jugo de naranja.

drive　　manejar

Mick is driving a dump truck.
Mick maneja un volquete.

drop¹　　la gota

two drops of water
dos gotas de agua

drop²　　dejar caer

Ellie has dropped her cake.
Ellie ha dejado caer su pastel.

drum　　el tambor

a red drum
un tambor rojo

dry¹　　secar, (yourself) secarse

Anna is drying herself with a blue towel.
Anna se seca con una toalla azul.

dry²　　seco

The clothes are dry.
La ropa está seca.

duck　　el pato

There is a duck on the water.
Hay un pato en el agua.

duckling　　el patito

How many ducklings are there?
¿Cuántos patitos hay?

dull　　(color) apagado, (story) aburrido

a dull green
un verde apagado

a dull book
un libro aburrido

a b c **d** e f g h i j k l m n o p q r s t u v w x y z

Ee

eagle *to* e-mail

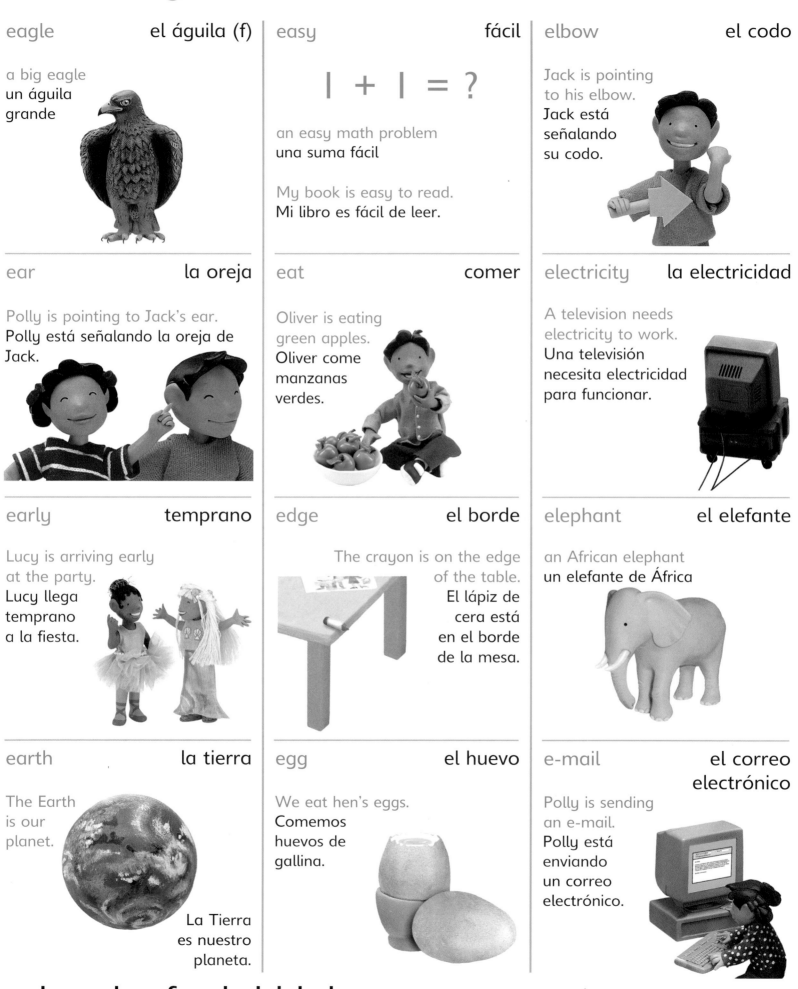

eagle   el águila (f)

a big eagle
un águila grande

ear   la oreja

Polly is pointing to Jack's ear.
Polly está señalando la oreja de Jack.

early   temprano

Lucy is arriving early at the party.
Lucy llega temprano a la fiesta.

earth   la tierra

The Earth is our planet.
La Tierra es nuestro planeta.

easy   fácil

$$1 + 1 = ?$$

an easy math problem
una suma fácil

My book is easy to read.
Mi libro es fácil de leer.

eat   comer

Oliver is eating green apples.
Oliver come manzanas verdes.

edge   el borde

The crayon is on the edge of the table.
El lápiz de cera está en el borde de la mesa.

egg   el huevo

We eat hen's eggs.
Comemos huevos de gallina.

elbow   el codo

Jack is pointing to his elbow.
Jack está señalando su codo.

electricity   la electricidad

A television needs electricity to work.
Una televisión necesita electricidad para funcionar.

elephant   el elefante

an African elephant
un elefante de África

e-mail   el correo electrónico

Polly is sending an e-mail.
Polly está enviando un correo electrónico.

a b c d e f g h i j k l m n o p q r s t u v w x y z

e

empty *to* eye

empty vacío

The cookie jar is empty.
El tarro de galletas está vacío.

end (story, time) **el fin,**
(table, line) **el extremo**

The End

enjoy (activity) **gustar*,**
(yourself) **divertirse**

Molly enjoys singing.
A Molly le gusta cantar.
She's enjoying herself.
Se divierte.

enormous enorme

an enormous blue whale
una enorme ballena azul

envelope el sobre

a pale green envelope

un sobre verde claro

equal igual

The two girls have equal amounts of sand.

Las dos niñas tienen cantidades iguales de arena.

escape escaparse

The black cat is escaping.
El gato negro se escapa.

even par

The pink bunny is jumping on the even numbers.
El conejo rosa salta en los números pares.

1 2 3 4 5 6 7

evening la tarde

The sun sets in the evening.

El sol se pone por la tarde.

expensive caro

The car is more expensive than the duck.

El coche es más caro que el pato.

explain explicar

Mr. Levy is explaining the math problems.
El señor Levy está explicando las sumas.

2+3 =
5+4 =
8+5 =

eye el ojo

Jack is pointing to Polly's eye.
Jack está señalando el ojo de Polly.

a b c d e f g h i j k l m n o p q r s t u v w x y z

* This verb is the other way around from English – as though you were saying "Singing pleases Molly".

Ff face *to* feel

face¹   la cara

This is Jack's face.

Ésta es la cara de Jack.

face²   estar enfrente

One giraffe is facing the other.

Una girafa está enfrente de la otra.

fact   el hecho

It is a fact that babies sleep a lot.

Es un hecho que los bebés duermen mucho.

fairy   el hada (f)

The fairy has a magic wand.

El hada tiene una varita mágica.

fall   caer, (over) caerse

When the clown falls, everyone laughs.

Cuando el payaso se cae, todo el mundo se ríe.

far   lejos

The butcher's store isn't far.

La carnicería no está lejos.

farm   la granja

There are sheep on this farm.
En esta granja hay ovejas.

farmer   el granjero

Mike is a farmer.

Mike es granjero.

fast   rápido

Eric goes very fast on his skis.
Eric va muy rápido en sus esquíes.

fat   gordo

a fat cat
un gato gordo

feed   dar de comer

Polly is feeding the hens.

Polly da de comer a las gallinas.

feel (touch) tocar, (happy or sad) sentirse

Feel this silk!
¡Toca esta seda!

Beth is feeling great.
Beth se siente de maravilla.

a b c d e **f** g h i j k l m n o p q r s t u v w x y z

fence   la valla

the backyard fence
la valla del jardín

few   poco

Becky has very few strawberries.
Becky tiene muy pocas fresas.

field   el campo

There are some cows in the field.
Hay unas vacas en el campo.

fight   pelearse

The children are fighting with cushions.

Los niños se pelean con unos cojines.

fill   llenar

Ivan fills his wheelbarrow with sand.
Ivan llena su carretilla de arena.

find   encontrar

Megan is finding crayons under the table.
Megan encuentra lápices de cera debajo de la mesa.

finger   el dedo

Jack is pointing to his finger.
Jack está señalando su dedo.

finish   terminar

Danny is finishing his drink.
Danny está terminando su bebida.

fire   el fuego, (house on fire) el incendio

a wood fire
un fuego de leña

fire engine   el coche de bomberos

The fire engine is new.
El coche de bomberos es nuevo.

firefighter   el bombero

Firefighters put out fires.
Los bomberos apagan los incendios.

first   primero

Jenny is first.
Jenny es la primera.

a b c d e f g h i j k l m n o p q r s t u v w x y z

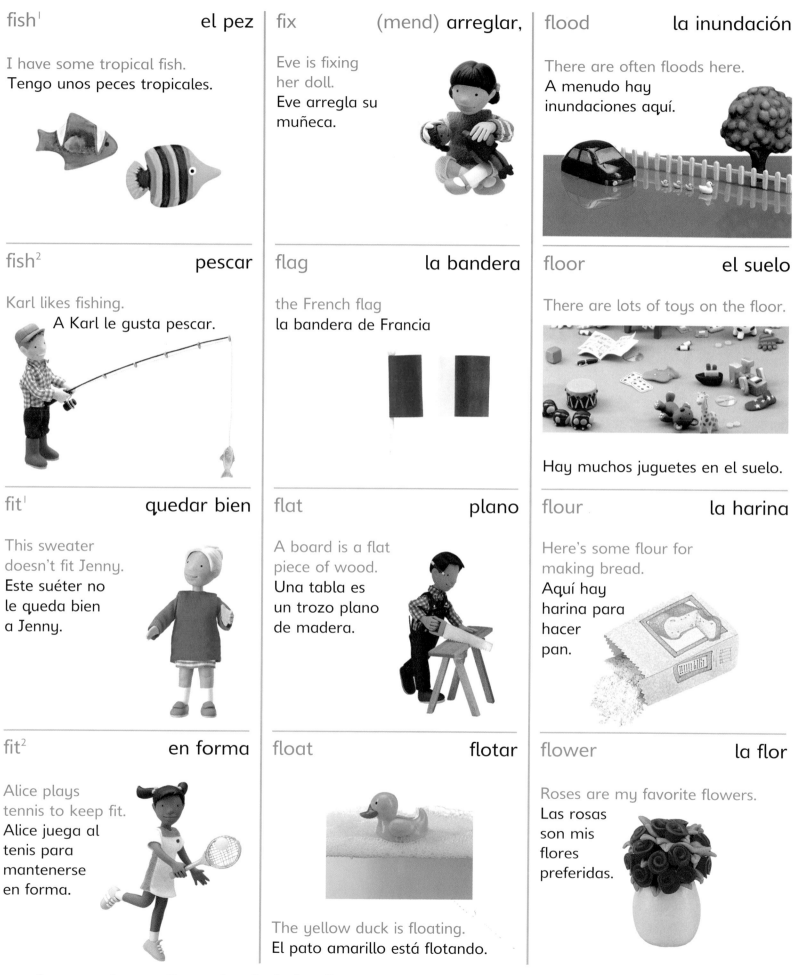

fish¹   el pez

I have some tropical fish.
Tengo unos peces tropicales.

fish²   pescar

Karl likes fishing.
A Karl le gusta pescar.

fit¹   quedar bien

This sweater doesn't fit Jenny.
Este suéter no le queda bien a Jenny.

fit²   en forma

Alice plays tennis to keep fit.
Alice juega al tenis para mantenerse en forma.

fix   (mend) arreglar,

Eve is fixing her doll.
Eve arregla su muñeca.

flag   la bandera

the French flag
la bandera de Francia

flat   plano

A board is a flat piece of wood.
Una tabla es un trozo plano de madera.

float   flotar

The yellow duck is floating.
El pato amarillo está flotando.

flood   la inundación

There are often floods here.
A menudo hay inundaciones aquí.

floor   el suelo

There are lots of toys on the floor.

Hay muchos juguetes en el suelo.

flour   la harina

Here's some flour for making bread.
Aquí hay harina para hacer pan.

flower   la flor

Roses are my favorite flowers.
Las rosas son mis flores preferidas.

a b c d e **f** g h i j k l m n o p q r s t u v w x y z

fly¹   la mosca

A fly is an insect.
La mosca es un insecto.

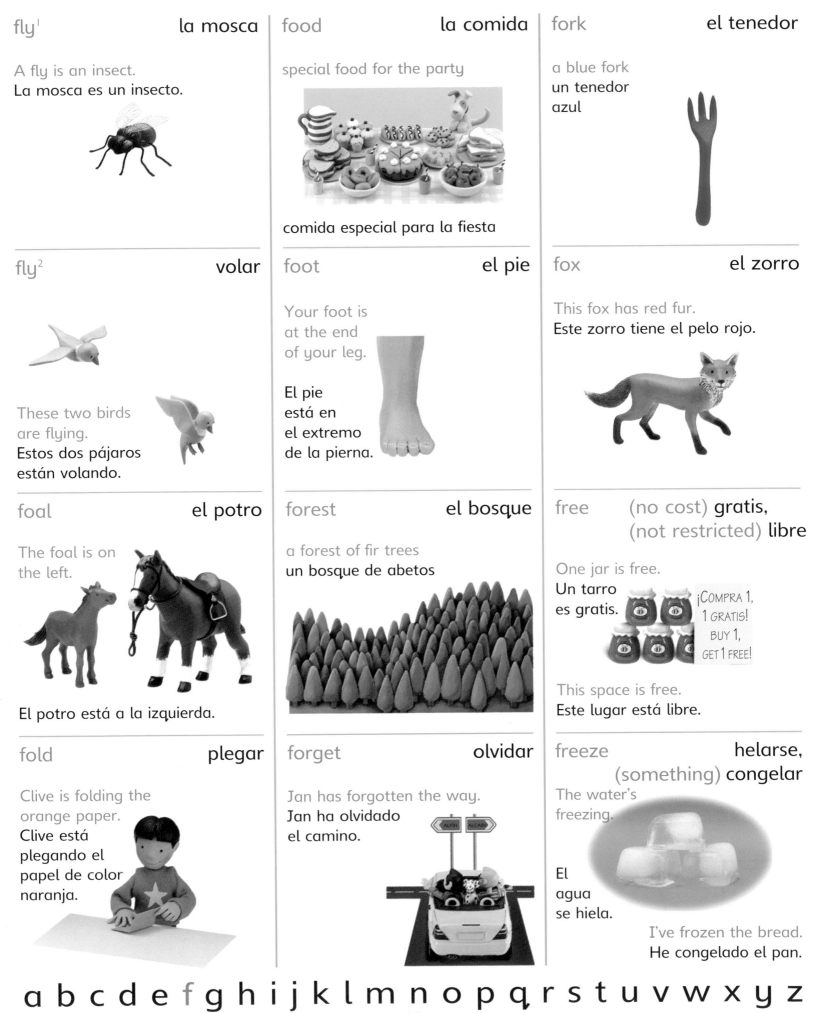

fly²   volar

These two birds are flying.
Estos dos pájaros están volando.

foal   el potro

The foal is on the left.

El potro está a la izquierda.

fold   plegar

Clive is folding the orange paper.
Clive está plegando el papel de color naranja.

food   la comida

special food for the party

comida especial para la fiesta

foot   el pie

Your foot is at the end of your leg.

El pie está en el extremo de la pierna.

forest   el bosque

a forest of fir trees
un bosque de abetos

forget   olvidar

Jan has forgotten the way.
Jan ha olvidado el camino.

fork   el tenedor

a blue fork
un tenedor azul

fox   el zorro

This fox has red fur.
Este zorro tiene el pelo rojo.

free   (no cost) gratis, (not restricted) libre

One jar is free.
Un tarro es gratis.

¡COMPRA 1, 1 GRATIS! BUY 1, GET 1 FREE!

This space is free.
Este lugar está libre.

freeze   helarse, (something) congelar

The water's freezing.

El agua se hiela.

I've frozen the bread.
He congelado el pan.

a b c d e f g h i j k l m n o p q r s t u v w x y z

freezer   el congelador

This freezer is filled with food.
Este congelador está lleno de comida.

fresh   fresco

Mrs. Martin sells fresh fruit.
La señora Martin vende fruta fresca.

friend   el amigo la amiga

Ellie's friends are coming to her party.

Los amigos de Ellie vienen a su fiesta.

friendly   simpático

Marco is very friendly.
Marco es muy simpático.

frog   la rana

This frog is from South America.
Esta rana es de América Latina.

front   delante

The front door is open.
La puerta de delante está abierta.

fruit   la fruta

some lovely fruit
unas frutas muy buenas

fry   freír

Dad is frying some eggs.
Papá fríe unos huevos.

full   lleno

Greg's cart is full.
El carrito de Greg está lleno.

fun   divertido

It's fun going on the merry-go-round.

Es divertido ir en el carrusel.

funny   gracioso, (strange) raro

Jack is telling a funny story.
Jack cuenta una historia graciosa.

a funny smell
un olor raro

fur   el pelo, (on clothes) la piel

This kitten has soft fur.
Este gatito tiene el pelo suave.

a fur cap
una gorra de piel

a b c d e **f** g h i j k l m n o p q r s t u v w x y z

game — el juego, el partido

a children's game
un juego de niños

a game of basketball
un partido de baloncesto

gentle — dulce, (animal) manso

Pip is a gentle dog.
Pip es un perro manso.

gift — el regalo

Becky has a birthday gift for Polly.
Becky tiene un regalo de cumpleaños para Polly.

garden — el jardín

There are lots of flowers in Aggie's garden.
Hay muchas flores en el jardín de Aggie.

gerbil — el jerbo

A gerbil is a small animal.
El jerbo es un animal pequeño.

giraffe — la jirafa

A giraffe is an African animal.
La jirafa es un animal africano.

gas — el gas

This balloon is filled with gas.
Este globo está lleno de gas.

ghost — el fantasma

I don't believe in ghosts.
No creo en los fantasmas.

girl — la niña

There are three girls here.
Aquí hay tres niñas.

gate — la puerta

The backyard gate is blue.
La puerta del jardín es azul.

giant — el gigante

a friendly giant
un gigante simpático

give — dar, (as gift) regalar

Ethan is giving Jenny some wagons.
Ethan da unos vagones a Jenny.

a b c d e f **g** h i j k l m n o p q r s t u v w x y z

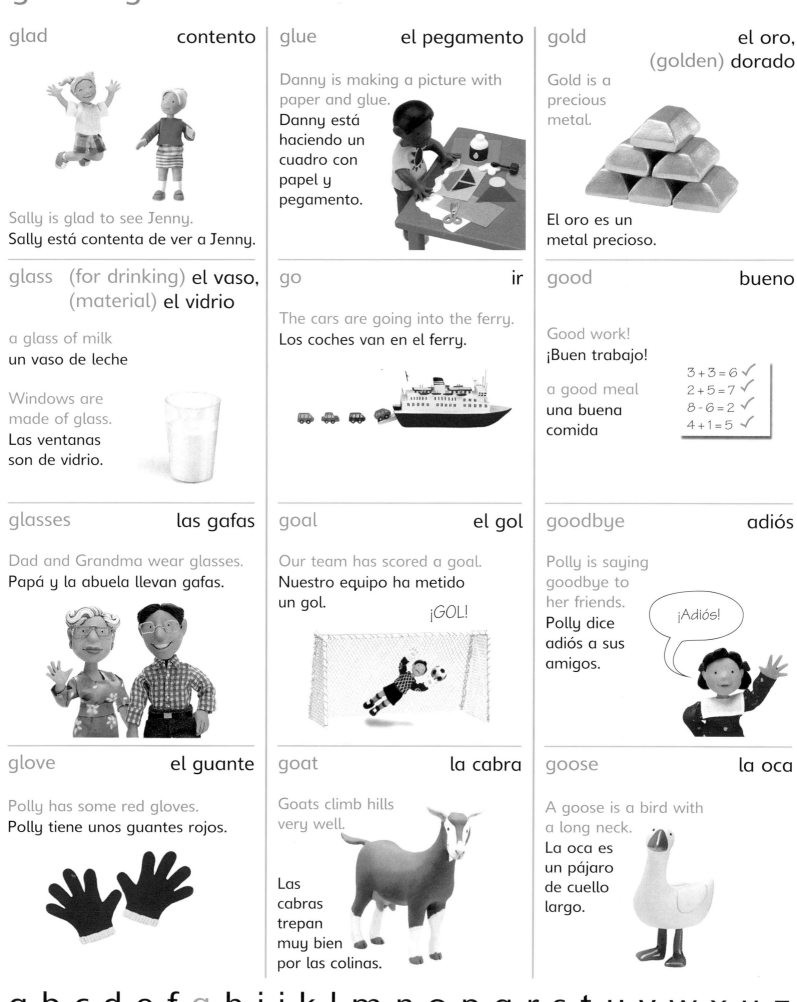

glad contento

Sally is glad to see Jenny.
Sally está contenta de ver a Jenny.

glass (for drinking) el vaso,
(material) el vidrio

a glass of milk
un vaso de leche

Windows are made of glass.
Las ventanas son de vidrio.

glasses las gafas

Dad and Grandma wear glasses.
Papá y la abuela llevan gafas.

glove el guante

Polly has some red gloves.
Polly tiene unos guantes rojos.

glue el pegamento

Danny is making a picture with paper and glue.
Danny está haciendo un cuadro con papel y pegamento.

go ir

The cars are going into the ferry.
Los coches van en el ferry.

goal el gol

Our team has scored a goal.
Nuestro equipo ha metido un gol.

¡GOL!

goat la cabra

Goats climb hills very well.
Las cabras trepan muy bien por las colinas.

gold el oro,
(golden) dorado

Gold is a precious metal.

El oro es un metal precioso.

good bueno

Good work!
¡Buen trabajo!

a good meal
una buena comida

3 + 3 = 6 ✓
2 + 5 = 7 ✓
8 - 6 = 2 ✓
4 + 1 = 5 ✓

goodbye adiós

Polly is saying goodbye to her friends.
Polly dice adiós a sus amigos.

¡Adiós!

goose la oca

A goose is a bird with a long neck.
La oca es un pájaro de cuello largo.

a b c d e f g h i j k l m n o p q r s t u v w x y z

grape — la uva

a bunch of grapes
un racimo
de uvas

grapefruit — el pomelo

I like grapefruit with sugar.
Me gustan los pomelos con
azúcar.

grass — la hierba

Cows and sheep eat grass.
Las vacas y las ovejas comen
hierba.

great (big) **gran, grande,**
(fantastic) **fantástico**

a great effort
un gran esfuerzo

a great day
at the beach
un día
fantástico
en la playa

ground — el suelo

Polly is looking at
ants on the ground.
Polly está mirando
unas hormigas
en el suelo.

group — el grupo

a group of children
un grupo de niños

grow — crecer

My plant is growing
very fast.
Mi planta crece
muy rápido.

grown-up (la persona)
mayor

Grown-ups are
always stopping
to talk.
Los
mayores
siempre
se paran
a charlar.

guess — adivinar

Is Polly going to guess
what's in the box?
¿Va a adivinar
Polly lo que
hay en la caja?

guest — el invitado
la invitada

Ellie is welcoming the
guests.

Ellie da la bienvenida a los
invitados.

guinea pig — el cobayo

A guinea pig is a small pet.
El cobayo es una mascota
pequeña.

guitar — la guitarra

A guitar is an
instrument
with six strings.

La guitarra
es un
instrumento
con seis
cuerdas.

a b c d e f g h i j k l m n o p q r s t u v w x y z

Hh   hair *to* hard

hair   **el pelo**

Rosie and Katie have fair hair.

Rosie y Katie tienen el pelo rubio.

hairbrush   **el cepillo**

I have a red hairbrush.
Tengo un cepillo rojo.

half   **el medio, la media,**
        (portion) **la mitad**

one and a half hours
una hora y media

half the bun
la mitad del panecillo

hamburger   **la hamburguesa**

Dad's making hamburgers.

Papa está haciendo unas hamburguesas.

hammer   **el martillo**

a hammer for doing carpentry
un martillo para hacer bricolaje

hamster   **el hámster**

Hamsters eat nuts and seeds.
Los hámsters comen nueces y semillas.

hand   **la mano**

This is Jack's left hand.
Ésta es la mano izquierda de Jack.

handle (door) **el picaporte,**
        (knife, pan) **el mango**

the door handle   el picaporte

The pan handle's broken.
El mango de la sartén está roto.

hang   **colgar**

Jack is hanging his jacket.
Jack está colgando su chaqueta.

happen   **pasar**

What's happening here?
¿Qué pasa acá?

happy   **feliz**

Sally is feeling very happy today.
Sally se siente muy feliz hoy.

hard   (surface) **duro,**
        (task) **difícil**

a hard job
un trabajo difícil

hard ground
un suelo duro

a b c d e f g **h** i j k l m n o p q r s t u v w x y z

hat — el sombrero

I have an orange hat with a flower.

Tengo un sombrero de color naranja con una flor.

hate — odiar

Maddy hates spiders.

Maddy odia a las arañas.

have — tener

Julia has some new red shoes.
Julia tiene unos zapatos rojos nuevos.

head — la cabeza

Polly's head is in the circle.
La cabeza de Polly está en el círculo.

hear — oír

Jack can hear the dog barking.

¡Guau guau!

Jack oye ladrar al perro.

heart — el corazón

My heart is beating fast.
Mi corazón late deprisa.

heart shaped
en forma de corazón

heat — calentar

Yvonne is heating coffee in the microwave.
Yvonne está calentando café en el microondas.

heavy — pesado

The boys are trying to move a heavy package.

Los chicos están intentando mover un paquete pesado.

height — la altura, (person) la estatura

Dad is checking Milo's height.
Papá está comprobando la estatura de Milo.

helicopter — el helicóptero

an emergency helicopter
un helicóptero de urgencias

hello — hola

Lisa is saying hello to her sister.

¡Hola!

Lisa dice hola a su hermana.

helmet — el casco

Grace wears a helmet for skateboarding.
Grace lleva casco para montar en monopatín.

a b c d e f g **h** i j k l m n o p q r s t u v w x y z

help   ayudar

Jack is helping his dad with the cooking.
Jack ayuda a su papá con la cocina.

highchair   la silla alta

Highchairs are for small children.
Las sillas altas son para los niños pequeños.

hold   sostener

Neil is holding the trophy.
Neil sostiene el trofeo.

hen   la gallina

Hens lay eggs.
Las gallinas ponen huevos.

hill   la colina

The house is at the top of the hill.
La casa está en lo alto de la colina.

hole   el agujero, (in the ground) el hoyo

This sweater has a hole in it.
Este suéter tiene un agujero.

hide   (things) esconder, (yourself) esconderse

The clown is hiding behind the armchair.
El payaso se esconde detrás del sillón.

hippopotamus *or* hippo   el hipopótamo

Hippos live in Africa.
Los hipopótamos viven en África.

home   la casa

This is our home.
Ésta es nuestra casa.

high   alto

The balloon is very high in the sky.
El globo va muy alto por el cielo.

a high building
un edificio alto

hit   golpear

Alice is hitting the ball with her racket.
Alice golpea la pelota con su raqueta.

honey   la miel

Honey is very sweet.
La miel es muy dulce.

a b c d e f g **h** i j k l m n o p q r s t u v w x y z

hop — **dar saltos**

Anna is hopping.

Anna está dando saltos.

hotdog — **el hot dog**

A hotdog is a sausage on a bun.
Un hot dog es una salchicha con un panecillo.

hug — **abrazar**

Nicholas is hugging his teddy bear.
Nicholas abraza a su osito.

horse — **el caballo**

Martin's horse is named Star.
El caballo de Martin se llama Star.

hotel — **el hotel**

Mr. Brand is spending his vacation at this hotel.
El señor Brand pasa sus vacaciones en este hotel.

HOTEL LUCIDA

(to be) hungry — **tener hambre**

Oliver is very hungry.
Oliver tiene mucha hambre.

hospital — **el hospital**

the new hospital
el hospital nuevo

hour — **la hora**

The short hand on the clock shows the hours.
La manecilla corta del reloj señala las horas.

hurry — **apurarse**

Jack and Polly are hurrying to catch the dog.
Jack y Polly se apuran para atrapar al perro.

hot — **caliente**

Careful, it's hot!

¡Cuidado, está caliente!

house — **la casa**

a house with a garden
una casa con jardín

hurt — **doler**

Ross is crying because his tummy hurts.
Ross está llorando porque le duele el estómago.

a b c d e f g **h** i j k l m n o p q r s t u v w x y z

Ii ice *to* itch

ice el hielo

ice cubes

cubitos de hielo

ice cream el helado

different flavors of ice cream
helados de
sabores
diferentes

idea la idea

¡Vamos a jugar en el parque!

Andy has an idea:
Let's go and play
in the park!

Andy tiene
una idea.

insect el insecto

All insects have six legs.

Todos los insectos
tienen seis patas.

inside dentro

The kitten is inside
the flowerpot.
El gatito está
dentro de
la maceta.

Let's go inside.
Vamos dentro.

instead en vez de

Hoy he hecho
té frío en vez de
jugo de fruta.

Mrs. Dot has made
iced tea instead of
fruit juice today.

Internet Internet (m)

Polly is searching the Internet.
Polly está buscando información
en Internet.

invitation la invitación

a party invitation una invitación
a una fiesta

Isabel te invita a su
Fiesta de Cumpleaños
el sábado 6 de abril
a las 4.30 h

invite invitar

Imogen is inviting Martin to
her party.
¿Quieres venir
a mi fiesta?

Imogen está
invitando a
Martin a
su fiesta.

iron la plancha

a steam iron
una plancha
de vapor

island la isla

a desert island
una isla desierta

itch picar

Fred's ear itches.
A Fred le pica
la oreja.

a b c d e f g h i j k l m n o p q r s t u v w x y z

Jj jacket *to* jungle

jacket   la chaqueta

Kathy is wearing
a yellow jacket.
Kathy lleva
una chaqueta
amarilla.

jar   el tarro

jars of honey, mustard and jelly
unos tarros de miel, mostaza
y mermelada

jeans   los vaqueros

new jeans
unos
vaqueros
nuevos

jigsaw   el rompecabezas

This jigsaw puzzle is easy.
Este rompecabezas es fácil.

job   el empleo

Aggie has a job.
She is a gardener.
Aggie tiene un
empleo. Es
jardinera.

join   (attach) unir,
(become a member)
hacerse socio

Ethan is joining
the wagons to
the train.
Ethan une los
vagones al tren.

I'm joining a club.
Me hago socio de un club.

joke   el chiste

Jack's joke:
El chiste de Jack:

¡Una abeja
dando marcha
atrás!

¿Qué animal
hace zzzb?

What animal
goes zzzub?
A bee going
backward!

journey   el viaje

a train journey
un viaje en tren

juggle   hacer malabarismos

The clown is juggling
with some toys.
El payaso
está haciendo
malabarismos
con unos
juguetes.

juice   el jugo

orange juice
jugo de
naranja

jump   saltar

Sally is jumping
because she's
happy.

Sally está
saltando
porque está
contenta.

jungle   la jungla

There are lots of plants and
animals in the jungle.
Hay muchas plantas y muchos
animales en la jungla.

a b c d e f g h i **j** k l m n o p q r s t u v w x y z

Kk kangaroo *to* kite

kangaroo   el canguro

A kangaroo is
an Australian
animal.
El canguro
es un animal
australiano.

keep   guardar,
conservar

Sam keeps his things
on the shelf.
Sam guarda
sus cosas en
el estante.

Keep the butter cold.
Conserva la mantequilla fría.

key   la llave

the front door key
la llave de la puerta
de entrada

kick   patear

Neil is
kicking
the ball.

Neil
patea
la pelota.

kid   el cabrito

a goat and her kid
una cabra y su
cabrito

kill   matar

The heat
has killed
my plant.

El calor ha
matado a mi planta.

kind¹   el tipo

different kinds of fruit
varios tipos de frutas

kind²   amable

Mr. Dot is kind.
He does his
neighbor's
shopping.
El señor
Dot es muy
amable. Hace
la compra
a su vecino.

king   el rey

Adam is dressed
up as a king.
Adam está
disfrazado
de rey.

kiss   besar

Polly is
kissing
Alex.
Polly
besa
a Alex.

kitchen   la cocina

Dad and Jack are in the kitchen.

Papá y Jack están en la cocina.

kite   la cometa

a red and yellow kite
una cometa roja
y amarilla

a b c d e f g h i j **k** l m n o p q r s t u v w x y z

kitten — **el gatito**

The kitten is playing with a ball of yarn.
El gatito está jugando con un ovillo de lana.

knight — **el caballero**

This knight has shiny armor.
Este caballero lleva una armadura brillante.

ladder — **la escalera**

a small ladder
una escalera pequeña

knee — **la rodilla**

This is Polly's right knee.
Ésta es la rodilla derecha de Polly.

knock — **golpear, (over) tirar**

Pip has knocked the chair over.
Pip ha tirado la silla.

lady — **la señora**

The two ladies are talking.
Las dos señoras están charlando.

kneel (down) **arrodillarse,** (be kneeling) **estar de rodillas**

Suzie is kneeling.
Suzie está de rodillas.

knot — **el nudo**

a simple knot
un nudo sencillo

ladybug — **la mariquita**

A ladybug is an insect.
La mariquita es un insecto.

knife — **el cuchillo**

I need a knife to cut the apple.
Necesito un cuchillo para cortar la manzana.

know (people) **conocer,** (facts) **saber**

Sam knows these children.
Sam conoce a estos niños.

I know he is angry.
Sé que está enojado.

lake — **el lago**

There is a small lake in the valley.
Hay un pequeño lago en el valle.

a b c d e f g h i j k l m n o p q r s t u v w x y z

lamb el cordero

A lamb is a baby sheep.
El cordero es la cría de la oveja.

lamp la lámpara

Here are two table lamps.
Aquí hay dos lámparas de mesa.

land la tierra

On this map, the land is brown.
En este mapa, la tierra es marrón.

language el lenguaje, (foreign) el idioma

Guten Tag!

Bonjour!

They can speak foreign languages.
Saben hablar idiomas extranjeros.

large grande

Becky is under a large tree.
Becky está debajo de un gran árbol.

last último

The black dog is last.
El perro negro es el último.

late (near the end) tarde, (not on time) con retraso

PLAZA MAYO

22

The bus is always late.
El autobús llega siempre con retraso.

late at night
tarde por la noche

laugh reírse

Jack and Polly are laughing.

¡Ja ja ja!

¡Ji ji ji!

Jack y Polly se están riendo.

lazy perezoso

a lazy cat
un gato perezoso

lead ir a la cabeza, (direction) conducir

The white duck is leading.

El pato blanco va a la cabeza.

This road leads to the village.
Esta carretera conduce al pueblo.

leaf la hoja

leaves from a tree

unas hojas de árbol

lean inclinarse

The tower leans to the right
La torre se inclina hacia la derecha.

a b c d e f g h i j k l m n o p q r s t u v w x y z

learn *to* lick

learn   **aprender**

Steve is learning
to play the guitar.
Steve aprende a
tocar la guitarra.

leave   **(a place) irse,
(something) dejar**

Mr. Bun is
leaving.
El señor
Bun se va.

I've left my bag at home.
He dejado mi bolsa en casa.

left   **izquierdo**

Lisa is holding
the crayon in
her left hand.
Lisa tiene el
lápiz de cera
en su mano
izquierda.

leg   **la pierna**

Tamsin wears tights so
her legs don't get cold.
Tamsin lleva
medias para no
tener frío en
las piernas.

lemon   **el limón**

seven
lemons

siete
limones

length   **el largo**

a ruler to measure the length
of the paper
una regla para medir el largo
del papel

less   **menos**

Ethan
has less ice cream than Olivia.
Ethan tiene menos helado
que Olivia.

lesson   **la lección**

Mr. Levy is giving a math lesson.

2 + 4 = 6

El señor
Levy
da una
lección de
aritmética.

let   **dejar**

Mr. Dot is letting
Jack mail the letter.
El señor
Dot deja
que Jack
eche su
carta.

letter   **la carta**

a letter to a friend
una carta a
una amiga

C/ Siesta 22
51500 Bostezo

31 de marzo

Querida María :

Muchísimas gracias por la
preciosa bolsa que me has
regalado. La llevo a la escuela
todos los días.

Un abrazo,

lettuce   **la lechuga**

Lettuce goes well in salads.
La lechuga va bien en las
ensaladas.

lick   **lamer**

Pip is licking Jack.

Pip está lamiendo a Jack.

a b c d e f g h i j k **l** m n o p q r s t u v w x y z

lid *to* lip

l

lid — la tapa

the lid of the mustard jar
la tapa del tarro de mostaza

lie¹ — (lie down) acostarse, (be lying) estar acostado

Kirsty is lying in bed.
Kirsty está acostada en su cama.

lie² — mentir

He's lying. — Está mintiendo.

¿Está ahí dentro?

No, no está.

life — la vida

Grandma and Granddad have had long, happy lives.
La abuela y el abuelo han tenido unas vidas largas y felices.

lift — levantar

The clown is pretending to lift something very heavy.
El payaso está fingiendo levantar algo muy pesado.

light¹ — la luz

This lamp gives a lot of light.
Esta lámpara da mucha luz.

Switch off the lights!
¡Apaga la luz!

light² — (color) claro, pálido, (not heavy) ligero

light pink
rosa pálido

light as a feather
ligero como una pluma

like¹ — gustar*

Becky likes strawberries.
A Becky le gustan las fresas.

like² — como

Sara has black hair, like her brother.
Sara tiene el pelo negro, como su hermano.

line — (on paper) la línea, (of people) la hilera

a line of soccer players
una hilera de futbolistas

lion — el león

A lion is a wild animal.
El león es un animal salvaje.

lip — el labio

Zach's top lip
el labio superior de Zach

a b c d e f g h i j k l m n o p q r s t u v w x y z

* This verb is the other way around from English – as though you were saying "Strawberries please Becky".

list   la lista

a list of first names
una lista de
nombres

Adam
Becky
Danny
Ellie
Katie
Maddy
Ross
Tony

live   vivir

The Dot family lives here.

La familia Dot vive aquí.

lock   la cerradura

I need the key for this lock.
Necesito la llave para esta
cerradura.

log   el tronco

a log for the fire
un tronco para
el fuego

long   largo

A giraffe has a
very long neck.
La jirafa tiene
un cuello muy
largo.

look   mirar

Polly is looking
at the clown.
Polly mira
al payaso.

lose   perder

I've lost my ticket.
He perdido mi boleto.

The boys have
lost the game.
Los chicos
han perdido
el partido.

(a) lot   mucho, mucha,
                  muchos, muchas

a lot of teddy bears
muchos ositos

loud   fuerte

The music is very loud.

La música está muy fuerte.

love   (people) querer,
              (things) encantar*

Beth loves taking a bath.
A Beth le encanta bañarse.

low   bajo

This bird is flying very low.
Este pájaro vuela muy bajo.

lunch   la comida

Sally has pizza
for lunch.
Sally toma
pizza a la
hora de la
comida.

a b c d e f g h i j k **l** m n o p q r s t u v w x y z
* This verb is the other way around from English – as though you were saying "Bathing delights Beth".

machine   la máquina

a sewing machine

una máquina de coser

magic   la magia

The clown is doing magic tricks.
El payaso hace trucos
de magia.

main   principal

the main
entrance of
the museum
la entrada
principal
del museo

make   hacer

Ethan is making
potato people.
Ethan hace
muñecos de papa.

man   el hombre

This man has
black hair.
Este hombre
tiene el pelo
negro.

many   muchos
muchas

There are
many
bees
on this
flower.

Hay
muchas
abejas en
esta flor.

map   el mapa

a map of the region
un mapa de la región

market   el mercado

the fruit and vegetable market
el mercado de frutas y verduras

match[1]   (game) **el partido,**
(for fire) **el fósforo**

a soccer match
un partido de fútbol

I have one match left.
Me queda un fósforo.

match[2]   hacer juego

These socks match.
Estos calcetines
hacen juego.

These socks
don't match.
Estos calcetines
no hacen juego.

matter   importar

Winning matters a lot to Neil and
his team.

A Neil y a su equipo les importa
mucho ganar.

meal   la comida

The meal is almost ready.
La comida está casi lista.

a b c d e f g h i j k l m n o p q r s t u v w x y z

mean — querer decir, significar

Mr. Levy is explaining what "x" means.
El señor Levy está explicando lo que quiere decir "x" *or* lo que significa "x".

measure — medir

Dad is measuring Milo's height.
Papá mide la estatura de Milo.

meat — la carne

Chicken is a kind of meat.
El pollo es un tipo de carne.

medicine — la medicina

cough medicine
medicina para la tos

meet (by chance) encontrarse, (by arrangement) quedar

I'm meeting Dad at six.
He quedado con papá a las seis.

Polly has met Lisa.
Polly se ha encontrado con Lisa.

mend — arreglar, (clothes) remendar

Robert is mending his shirt.
Robert está remendando la camisa.

mess — el desorden

What a mess!
¡Qué desorden!

message — el mensaje

There's a message for Mrs. Dot to call Paula.
Hay un mensaje para la señora Dot.

Mamá, llama a Paula, por favor.

metal — el metal

This bucket is made of metal.
Este cubo es de metal.

microwave — el microondas

a new microwave

un microondas nuevo

middle — el medio

The bear is in the middle of the grass.
El oso está en el medio de la hierba.

milk — la leche

fresh milk
leche fresca

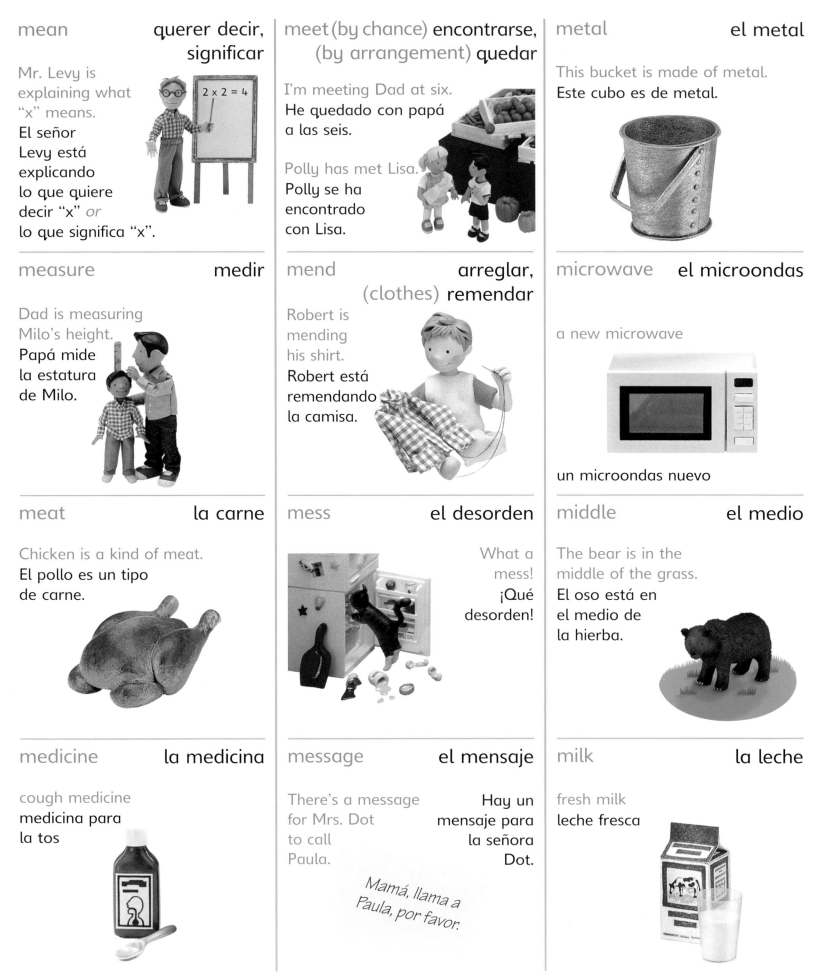

a b c d e f g h i j k l m n o p q r s t u v w x y z

mind *to* more

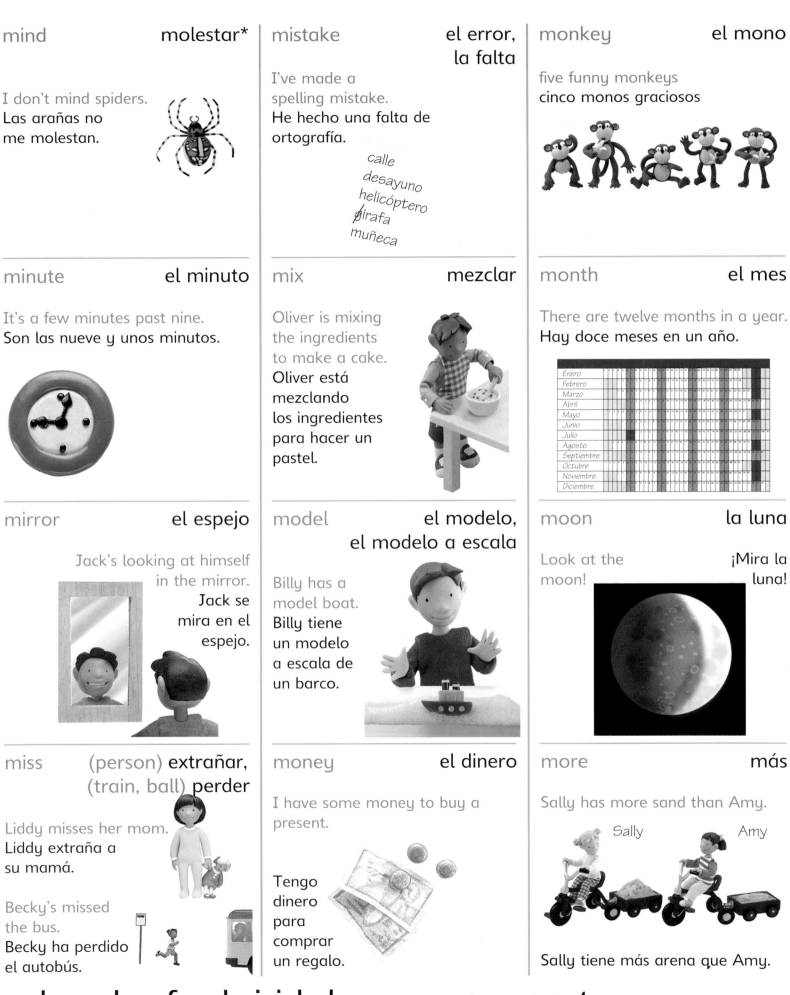

m

mind — molestar*

I don't mind spiders.
Las arañas no me molestan.

mistake — el error, la falta

I've made a spelling mistake.
He hecho una falta de ortografía.

calle
desayuno
helicóptero
girafa
muñeca

monkey — el mono

five funny monkeys
cinco monos graciosos

minute — el minuto

It's a few minutes past nine.
Son las nueve y unos minutos.

mix — mezclar

Oliver is mixing the ingredients to make a cake.
Oliver está mezclando los ingredientes para hacer un pastel.

month — el mes

There are twelve months in a year.
Hay doce meses en un año.

Enero
Febrero
Marzo
Abril
Mayo
Junio
Julio
Agosto
Septiembre
Octubre
Noviembre
Diciembre

mirror — el espejo

Jack's looking at himself in the mirror.
Jack se mira en el espejo.

model — el modelo, el modelo a escala

Billy has a model boat.
Billy tiene un modelo a escala de un barco.

moon — la luna

Look at the moon!   ¡Mira la luna!

miss — (person) extrañar, (train, ball) perder

Liddy misses her mom.
Liddy extraña a su mamá.

Becky's missed the bus.
Becky ha perdido el autobús.

money — el dinero

I have some money to buy a present.
Tengo dinero para comprar un regalo.

more — más

Sally has more sand than Amy.
Sally   Amy
Sally tiene más arena que Amy.

a b c d e f g h i j k l m n o p q r s t u v w x y z

* This verb is the other way around from English – as though you were saying "Spiders don't bother me".

morning — la mañana

a summer morning
una mañana de verano

mountain — la montaña

Mountains are higher than hills.
Las montañas son más altas
que las colinas.

much — mucho, mucha,
muchos, muchas

Mrs. Moon hasn't done much shopping.
La señora Moon no ha hecho muchas compras.

most — el más, la más,
los más, las más

Which of these caterpillars
has the most stripes?

¿Cuál de estas orugas
es la más rayada?

mouse — el ratón

a house mouse
un ratón
doméstico

a computer mouse
un ratón de
computadora

mud — el barro

Sally is covered in mud.
Sally está cubierta de barro.

moth — la mariposa
nocturna

Moths fly toward lights.

Las
mariposas
nocturnas vuelan hacia la luz.

mouth — la boca

Jack is pointing to Polly's mouth.
Jack está señalando la boca de Polly.

mushroom — el champiñón

Mushrooms are good to eat.
Los champiñones son ricos.

motorcycle — la moto

This is Steve's new motorcycle.

Ésta es la moto nueva de Steve.

move — mover

The crane is moving the crate.
La grua está moviendo la caja.

Don't move!   ¡No te muevas!

music — la música

Steve, Marco and Molly love music.
A Steve, a Marco y a Molly les encanta la música.

a b c d e f g h i j k l m n o p q r s t u v w x y z

Nn nail *to* nest

nail (metal) **el clavo,** (fingernail) **la uña**

I need some nails to fix the chair.
Necesito unos clavos para arreglar la silla.

nail polish
esmalte de uñas

---

name **el nombre**

Polly is choosing a name for her tiger.
Polly elige un nombre para su tigre.

---

narrow **estrecho**

The gap is so narrow that the kitten can't fit through.
El hueco es tan estrecho que el gatito no puede pasar.

---

nature **la naturaleza**

Polly is interested in nature.
Polly está interesada en la naturaleza.

---

naughty **travieso**

That naughty dog has stolen Jack's cake.
Ese perro travieso ha robado el pastel de Jack.

---

near **cerca**

The school is near the river.
La escuela está cerca del río.

---

neck **el cuello**

A giraffe has a very long neck.
La jirafa tiene un cuello muy largo.

---

necklace **el collar**

Ruth has a pretty necklace.
Ruth tiene un collar bonito.

---

need **necesitar,** (to do something) **tener que**

Sam needs to sleep.
Sam necesita dormir.

---

needle **la aguja**

a sewing needle
una aguja de coser

knitting needles
unas agujas de tejer

---

neighbor **el vecino la vecina**

These two people are neighbors.
Estas dos personas son vecinos.

---

nest **el nido**

Birds build nests for their eggs.
Los pájaros construyen nidos para sus huevos.

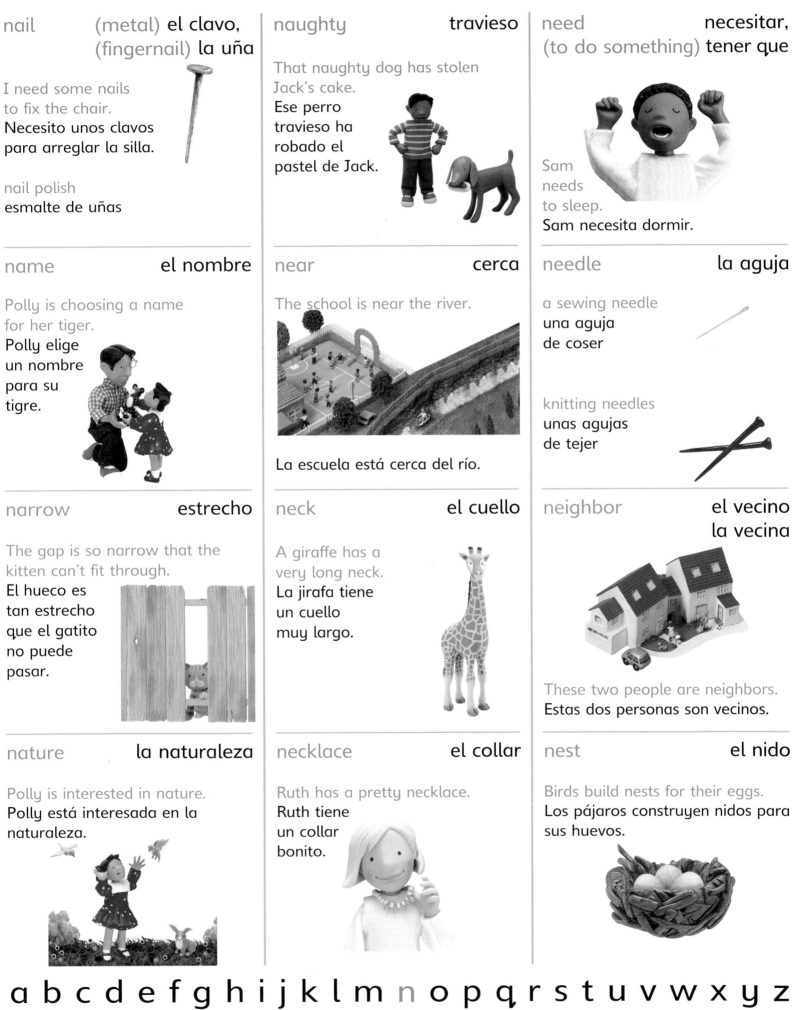

a b c d e f g h i j k l m n o p q r s t u v w x y z

net[1]   la red

Julia has a small fishing net.
Julia tiene una pequeña red de pesca.

The ball is caught in the net.
La pelota está atrapada en la red.

Net[2]   la Red

Polly is searching the Net.
Polly busca información en la Red.

never   nunca

The mailman never smiles.
El cartero no sonríe nunca.

new   nuevo

Julia has some new shoes.
Julia tiene unos zapatos nuevos.

news   las noticias

Mrs. Beef has some bad news: Oscar has disappeared.
La señora Beef tiene malas noticias.

¡Oscar se ha perdido!

newspaper   el periódico

This is Dad's newspaper.
Éste es el periódico de papá.

next   (beside) **al lado,** (after that) **después,** (next week) **próximo**

The yellow car is next to the red car.
El coche amarillo está al lado del coche rojo.

nice   (person) **simpático,** (to look at) **bonito**

Danny has made a very nice picture.
Danny ha hecho un cuadro muy bonito.

night   la noche

It's night time.   **Es de noche.**

nod   asentir con la cabeza

The dog is nodding.
El perro asiente con la cabeza.

noise   el ruido

This baby is making a lot of noise.
Este bebé hace mucho ruido.

¡GUA!

noisy   ruidoso

The boys are very noisy.
Los chicos son muy ruidosos.

a b c d e f g h i j k l m **n** o p q r s t u v w x y z

nose *to* nut

nose   la nariz

Polly is pointing to
Jack's nose.
Polly está
señalando
la nariz
de Jack.

note   la nota

a note for Mr. Dot
una nota para
el señor Dot

a low note
una nota
baja

*dentista
10.30 h*

notebook   el cuaderno

This is Jack's notebook.
Éste es el cuaderno de Jack.

NOTAS

notice   darse cuenta

The clown is hiding and
Annie hasn't noticed.
El payaso se
ha escondido
y Annie no
se ha dado
cuenta.

now   ahora

The clown is
holding a pie...
El payaso sostiene
una tarta...

...now he falls
down in it.
...ahora se cae
encima de ella.

number   el número,
(figure) la cifra

My phone number is ten
numbers long.

(012) 345-6789

Mi número de teléfono tiene
diez cifras.

nurse   el enfermero
la enfermera

The nurse is
pushing Sally
in a wheelchair.   La
enfermera
está
empujando
a Sally en
una silla
a ruedas.

nut   (walnut) la nuez,
(hazelnut) la avellana,
(almond) la almendra,
(peanut) el cacahuate,
el maní

ocean   el océano

An ocean is a huge sea.

Un océano es un mar enorme.

o'clock   la hora, las horas
(not usually said)

one o'clock in
the afternoon
la una de
la tarde

seven
o'clock in
the morning
las siete de la mañana

octopus   el pulpo

An octopus has eight tentacles.

El pulpo tiene ocho tentáculos.

odd   (number) impar,
(strange) raro

The blue bunny is jumping
on the odd numbers.
El conejo azul salta en los
números impares.

1   2   3   4   5

That's odd.   ¡Qué raro!

a b c d e f g h i j k l m n o p q r s t u v w x y z

often   a menudo

Mr. Dot and Jack
often go and
do the shopping.
El señor Dot
y Jack van a
menudo a
hacer la
compra.

oil   el aceite

Sunflower oil is
good for cooking.
El aceite de girasol
es bueno para
cocinar.

old   viejo

an old man
un hombre viejo

an old shoe
un zapato
viejo

once   una vez

They've been on
a balloon ride once.
Han hecho un
viaje en globo
una vez.

Once upon a time...
Había una vez...

onion   la cebolla

An onion has a strong taste.
La cebolla tiene un gusto fuerte.

only   sólo, solamente

Becky only has
two strawberries.
Becky sólo
tiene dos fresas
or Becky
solamente tiene
dos fresas.

open[1]   abrir

Mr. Dot is opening
the front door.
El señor Dot abre
la puerta de entrada.

Mrs. Dot is
opening the box.
La señora Dot
abre la caja.

open[2]   abierto

Mrs. Bird's store is open on
Saturdays.
La tienda de
la señora
Bird está
abierta los
sábados.

opposite[1]   opuesto

"Big" and "small" are
opposite words.
"Grande" y
"pequeño"
son palabras
opuestas.

opposite[2]   enfrente

Becky is sitting
opposite her teddy.
Becky está sentada
enfrente de su osito.

orange   la naranja, (color) (de color) naranja

a juicy
orange   una naranja jugosa

orange paint
pintura de
color naranja

other   otro

¿Tienes otros juguetes?

Pues, no.

Jenny's asking if Ethan has any
other toys.

a b c d e f g h i j k l m n **o** p q r s t u v w x y z

54

outside — fuera, afuera

The monkey is outside the box.
El mono está fuera de la caja.

Let's go and play outside!
¡Vamos a jugar afuera!

over (above) sobre, (finished) terminado

The bird is flying over the tree
El pájaro está volando sobre el árbol.

The party is over.
La fiesta ha terminado.

owl — el búho

Owls come out at night.
Los búhos salen de noche.

own — propio

Mrs. Bird has her own store.
La señora Bird tiene tienda propia.

page — la página

Polly is looking at the words on the page.
Polly mira las palabras en la página.

paint¹ — la pintura

bottles of paint
unas botellas de pintura

paint² — pintar

Shelley is painting an orange cat.
Shelley está pintando un gato naranja.

I am painting my bedroom.
Estoy pintando mi habitación.

pair — el par

a pair of striped socks
un par de calcetines a rayas.

palace — el palacio

a palace with golden domes
un palacio con cúpulas doradas

pale — claro, pálido

pale blue
azul claro

pale green
verde claro

pale yellow
amarillo pálido

paper — el papel, (newspaper) el periódico

writing paper
papel de escribir

parachute — el paracaídas

Mr. Brand is doing a parachute jump.
El señor Brand hace un salto en paracaídas.

a b c d e f g h i j k l m o p q r s t u v w x y z

parents — los padres

Mr. and Mrs. Dot are Polly and Jack's parents.
El señor y la señora Dot son los padres de Polly y Jack.

park¹ — el parque

Let's go and play in the park!
¡Vamos a jugar en el parque!

park² — estacionar

Jan parks here.
Jan estaciona aquí.

PARKING
12 PLAZAS

parrot — el loro

There are some parrots that can talk.
Hay loros que saben hablar.

part — la parte

A wheel is part of a car.
Una rueda es parte de un coche.

party — la fiesta

There are lots of guests at Ellie's party.
Hay muchos invitados en la fiesta de Ellie.

pass — pasar

They are passing the bank.
Están pasando por delante del banco.

Can you pass me the salt?
¿Me puedes pasar la sal?

past¹ — el pasado

clothes from the past
ropa del pasado

past² — por delante

They run past the stores.
Pasan corriendo por delante de las tiendas.

path — el sendero

This path goes to the village.
Este sendero va al pueblo.

paw — la zarpa

This is the tiger's paw.
Ésta es la zarpa del tigre.

pay — pagar

Ethan is paying for the apple.
Ethan paga la manzana.

a b c d e f g h i j k l m n o p q r s t u v w x y z

pea   el chícharo, la arveja

Peas are small, round vegetables.

Los chícharos son unas verduras pequeñas y redondas.

pear   la pera

a nice, sweet, green pear
una rica pera verde y dulce

penguin   el pingüino

Penguins live in Antarctica.
Los pingüinos viven en el Antártico.

peach   el melocotón

This peach is delicious.
Este melocotón es riquísimo.

pebble   el guijarro

There are lots of pebbles on the beach.

Hay muchos guijarros en la playa.

people   la gente

These people are waiting for the movie to start.

La gente está esperando a que empiece la película.

peak (mountain) la cumbre, (cap) la visera

There is snow on the peak.
Hay nieve en la cumbre.

a cap with a peak
una gorra de visera

pen   la pluma

This is my new pen.
Ésta es mi pluma nueva.

pepper (spice) la pimienta, (vegetable) el ají

a pepper mill
un molinillo de pimienta

green, red and yellow peppers
unos ajíes rojos, verdes y amarillos

peanut   el cacahuate, el maní

a packet of salted peanuts
un paquete de cacahuates salados

pencil   el lápiz

I am drawing in pencil.
Estoy dibujando con lápiz.

person   la persona

There is only one person here.
Aquí solamente hay una persona.

a b c d e f g h i j k l m n o p q r s t u v w x y z

pet — la mascota

some pets
unas
mascotas

phone — el teléfono

a yellow phone
un teléfono amarillo

photo — la fotografía

Polly is looking
at some
photos.

Polly está
mirando unas fotografías.

piano — el piano

Polly has a little, pink piano.
Polly tiene un pequeño piano rosa.

pick (choose) elegir,
(flowers, fruit) recoger

Oliver has
picked an
apple and
a cupcake.

Oliver ha
elegido una
manzana y
un pastel.

I'm picking some flowers.
Estoy recogiendo unas flores.

picnic — el picnic

Amy is having a picnic.
Amy está
haciendo
un picnic.

picture — el cuadro

Shelley's painted a
very nice picture.
Shelley ha
hecho un
cuadro muy
bonito.

piece — el pedazo,
la pieza

a jigsaw
puzzle
with
nine
pieces

un rompecabezas
con nueve piezas

pillow — la almohada

a big, soft pillow
una almohada grande y blanda

pilot — el piloto
la piloto

Jim wants to
be a pilot.
Jim quiere
ser piloto.

pineapple — la piña

A pineapple is a tropical fruit.
La piña es una fruta tropical.

pizza — la pizza

a vegetarian pizza
una pizza vegetariana

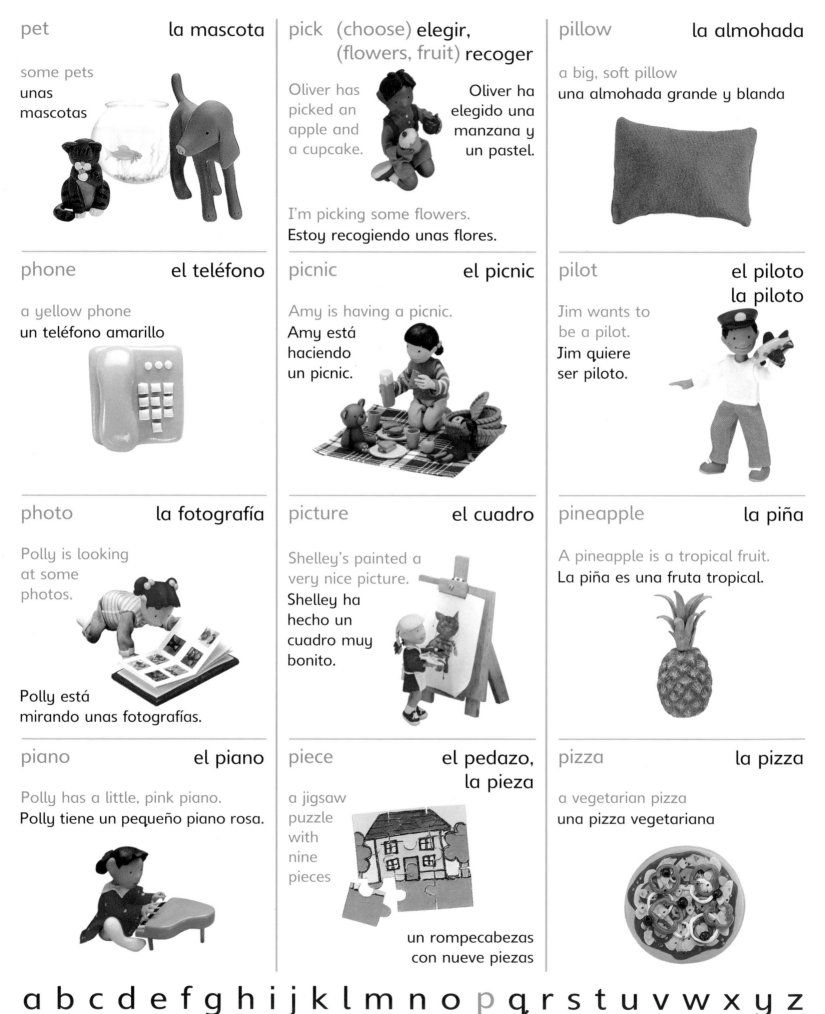

a b c d e f g h i j k l m n o p q r s t u v w x y z

place — el sitio

a good place to have lunch
un buen sitio para la comida

plan¹ — el plano

a plan of the first floor

el dormitorio
la sala de estar
el baño

un plano del primer piso

plan² — planear

Fecha: el 22 de septiembre
Invitados:
Alex
Becky
Danny
Ellie

Mrs. Dot is planning a party.
La señora Dot está planeando una fiesta.

plane — el avión

The plane is landing.
El avión está aterrizando.

planet — el planeta

a planet with rings
un planeta con anillos

plant — la planta

a house plant
una planta de interior

plate — el plato

My plate is clean.
Mi plato está limpio.

play — jugar, (music) tocar

Neil is playing soccer.
Neil está jugando al fútbol.

Polly is playing the piano.
Polly toca el piano.

playground (school) el patio de recreo, (park) la zona de recreo

the playground in the park
la zona de recreo en el parque

please — por favor

Becky is asking if she can please have some more strawberries.

¿Puedo tomar más fresas por favor?

plum — la ciruela

a nice, ripe plum
una buena ciruela madura

pocket — el bolsillo

Renata is putting her hands in her pockets.
Renata mete las manos en los bolsillos.

a b c d e f g h i j k l m n o **p** q r s t u v w x y z

poem — el poema

Shelley has written a poem about her cat.
Shelley ha escrito un poema sobre su gato.

Mi gato

Anda sin ruido
y sale de excursión.
De vuelta en la casa
duerme en un sillón.

Se lava la cara
todos los días.
Araña su plato
y pide comida.

Mi gato querido
es un buen amigo.

point¹ — (sharp) la punta, (score) el punto

the pencil point
la punta del lápiz

We're playing a game, and I already have forty points.
Estamos jugando y ya tengo cuarenta puntos.

point² — señalar

Polly is pointing to Jack's nose.
Polly está señalando la nariz de Jack.

police — la policía

Brian works for the police.
Brian trabaja en la policía.

police car — el coche de policía

There is no one in the police car.
No hay nadie en el coche de policía.

pond — la laguna

There is a duck on the pond.
Hay un pato en la laguna.

pony — el poney

a small pony
un poney pequeño

pool — la piscina

There's a children's pool in the park.
Hay una piscina infantil en el parque.

poor — pobre

rich people and poor people
los ricos y los pobres

Poor Ross, his tummy hurts.
Pobre Ross, le duele el estómago.

potato — la papa

Potatoes grow underground.
Las papas crecen bajo tierra.

present — el regalo

a surprise present for Polly
un regalo sorpresa para Polly

press — presionar

Danny is pressing down the blue paper with his hands.
Danny está presionando el papel azul con las manos.

a b c d e f g h i j k l m n o p q r s t u v w x y z

pretend — fingir

Nicholas is pretending to be asleep.

Nicholas finge estar dormido.

pretty — bonito

Anya has a pretty red dress.
Anya lleva un bonito vestido rojo.

price — el precio

The watermelons are two for the price of one.

2 por el precio de 1

prince — el príncipe

a brave prince
un príncipe valiente

princess — la princesa

a beautiful princess
una bella princesa

prize — el premio, (sports) el trofeo

Neil's team has won the prize.
El equipo de Neil ha ganado el trofeo.

promise — prometer

Prometo llevarte al parque.

Minnie's dad is promising to take her to the park.

puddle — el charco

Alex is jumping in the puddles.
Alex está saltando en los charcos.

pull — tirar

Jack is pulling the package.

Thomas   Jack

Jack tira del paquete.

pumpkin — la calabaza

A pumpkin is a large fruit.
La calabaza es una fruta grande.

pupil — el alumno la alumna

Mr. Levy and his pupils

El señor Levy y sus alumnos

puppet — el títere, la marioneta

This puppet has funny clothes.

Esta marioneta lleva una ropa muy graciosa.

a b c d e f g h i j k l m n o p q r s t u v w x y z

puppy — el cachorro

The yellow dog has a very sweet puppy.

El perro amarillo tiene un cachorro muy gracioso.

push — empujar

Thomas is pushing the package.

Thomas

Jack

Thomas empuja el paquete.

put — (put down) poner, (inside something) meter

Oliver is putting the bottle on the table.
Oliver está poniendo la botella en la mesa.

puzzle — el rompecabezas

This isn't a difficult puzzle.
No es un rompecabezas difícil.

quack — graznar

Ducks quack.
Los patos graznan.

¡Quac quac!

quarter — el cuarto, la cuarta parte

quarter past three
las tres y cuarto

a quarter of the cake
la cuarta parte del pastel

queen — la reina

Joy is dressed up as a queen.
Joy está disfrazada de reina.

question — la pregunta

Polly has a question: what's the clown's name?

¿Cómo te llamas?

Polly tiene una pregunta.

quick — rápido

Grace is very quick on her skateboard.
Grace va muy rápido en su monopatín.

quiet — (sound) suave, (silent) silencioso

Anna is so quiet that Milo doesn't hear her.
Anna es tan silenciosa que Milo no la oye.

quite — (fairly) bastante, (completely) del todo

I'm quite tired.
Estoy bastante cansado.

Mr. Bun hasn't quite finished.
El señor Bun no ha terminado del todo.

quiz — el cuestionario

This is a quiz about animals.
Éste es un cuestionario sobre animales.

Los animales
1) ¿Cual es el animal más grande del mundo?
2) ¿Qué tipo de animal es el tucán?
3) ¿A qué lugar del mundo irías para ver avestruces y leopardos?

a b c d e f g h i j k l m n o **p q** r s t u v w x y z

Rr rabbit *to* real

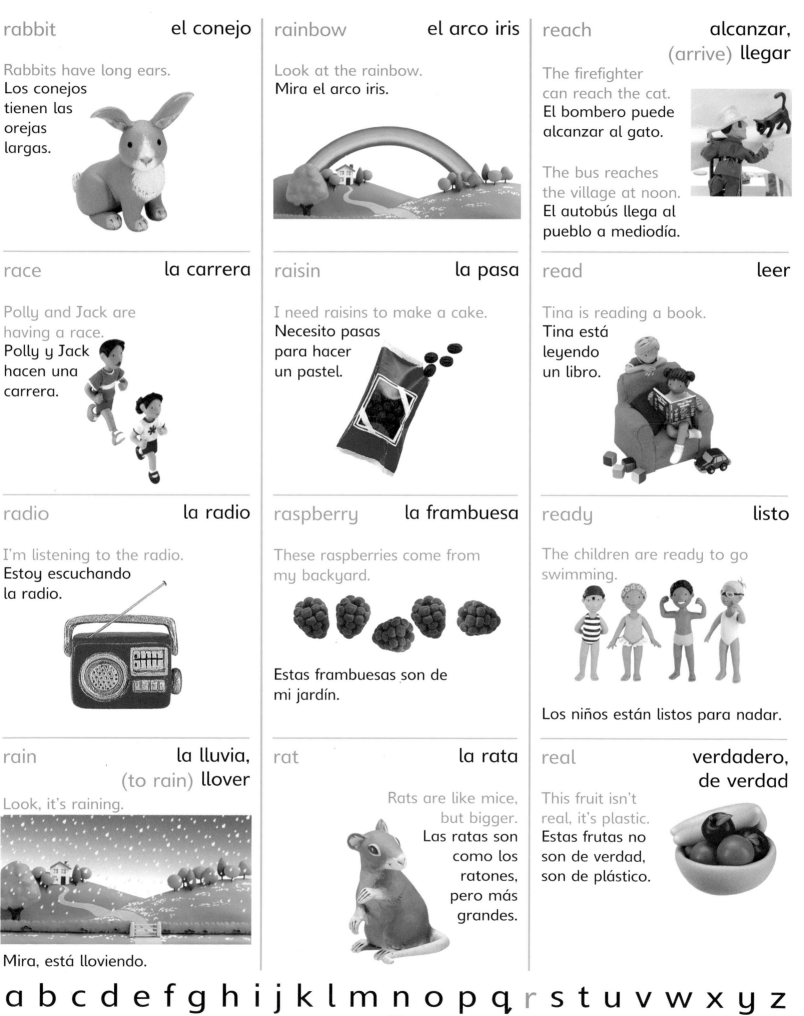

rabbit el conejo

Rabbits have long ears.
Los conejos tienen las orejas largas.

rainbow el arco iris

Look at the rainbow.
Mira el arco iris.

reach alcanzar, (arrive) llegar

The firefighter can reach the cat.
El bombero puede alcanzar al gato.

The bus reaches the village at noon.
El autobús llega al pueblo a mediodía.

race la carrera

Polly and Jack are having a race.
Polly y Jack hacen una carrera.

raisin la pasa

I need raisins to make a cake.
Necesito pasas para hacer un pastel.

read leer

Tina is reading a book.
Tina está leyendo un libro.

radio la radio

I'm listening to the radio.
Estoy escuchando la radio.

raspberry la frambuesa

These raspberries come from my backyard.
Estas frambuesas son de mi jardín.

ready listo

The children are ready to go swimming.
Los niños están listos para nadar.

rain la lluvia, (to rain) llover

Look, it's raining.
Mira, está lloviendo.

rat la rata

Rats are like mice, but bigger.
Las ratas son como los ratones, pero más grandes.

real verdadero, de verdad

This fruit isn't real, it's plastic.
Estas frutas no son de verdad, son de plástico.

a b c d e f g h i j k l m n o p q **r** s t u v w x y z

recorder — la flauta

I'm learning to play the recorder at school.

Estoy aprendiendo a tocar la flauta en la escuela.

rescue — rescatar

Mr. Sparks has rescued the cat.

El señor Sparks ha rescatado al gato.

rich — rico

Natalie is a very rich singer.

Natalie es una cantante muy rica.

refrigerator — la nevera, la heladera

The refrigerator is full of food.

La nevera está llena de comida.

rhinoceros — el rinoceronte *or* rhino

Rhinos live in hot countries.

Los rinocerontes viven en países calientes.

ride — (bicycle) ir en bicicleta, (horse) montar a caballo

Martin can ride.

Martin sabe montar a caballo.

remember — acordarse

Fiona can remember the date of her friend's birthday.

Fiona se acuerda del día de cumpleaños de su amiga.

El día de tu cumpleaños es el 26 de mayo.

ribbon — la cinta

Becky has green ribbons.

Becky lleva unas cintas verdes.

right — (not left) derecho, (not wrong) correcto

Greta has put the puppet on her right hand.

Greta ha puesto el títere en su mano derecha.

That's the right answer.

Ésa es la respuesta correcta.

reply — contestar

¿Quieres ir al parque?

Sí, por favor.

Minnie is replying to her dad.

Minnie contesta a su papá.

rice — el arroz

I prefer rice over pasta.

Prefiero el arroz a la pasta.

ring¹ — el anillo

a ring with a red stone

un anillo con una piedra roja

the rings of Saturn

los anillos de Saturno

a b c d e f g h i j k l m n o p q r s t u v w x y z

ring² sonar

The phone's ringing.
El teléfono suena.

¡rrring!

ripe maduro

The melon, the avocado and the watermelon are all ripe.

El melón, el aguacate y la sandía están maduros.

river el río

The houses are near the river.
Las casas están cerca del río.

road el camino

The road goes into town.
El camino va a la ciudad.

robot el robot

a toy robot
un robot de juguete

rock (stone) la roca, (music) el rock

There are rocks on the beach.
Hay unas rocas en la playa.

Steve likes playing rock.
A Steve le gusta tocar música rock.

rocket el cohete

a toy rocket
un cohete de juguete.

roof el tejado

The roof of this building is blue.
El tejado de este edificio es azul.

room (space) el lugar, (in house) la habitación

On this plan, there are six rooms.
En este plano, hay seis habitaciones.

Is there some room for me?
¿Hay lugar para mí?

rope la cuerda

Jack needs a rope to pull the package.

Jack necesita una cuerda para tirar del paquete.

rose la rosa

Roses are my favorite flowers.
Las rosas son mis flores preferidas.

round redondo

In general, drums are round.

En general, los tambores son redondos.

a b c d e f g h i j k l m n o p q **r** s t u v w x y z

rug   la alfombra

a red, yellow and blue rug
una alfombra roja, amarilla y azul

ruler   la regla

A ruler is useful for drawing straight lines.
Una regla es útil para dibujar líneas rectas.

run   correr

Polly and Jack are running.
Polly y Jack están corriendo.

rush   precipitarse, (correr) a toda prisa

They are rushing after Pip.
Corren a toda prisa detrás de Pip.

sad   triste

Liddy is sad without her mom.
Liddy está triste sin su mamá.

saddle   la silla (de montar)

Martin's horse has a new saddle.
El caballo de Martin tiene una silla nueva.

safe   seguro

a safe place to cross the street
un sitio seguro para cruzar la calle

sailor   el marinero

Gareth is dressed up as a sailor.
Gareth está disfrazado de marinero.

salad   la ensalada

a mixed salad
una ensalada mixta

salami   el salame

This is Italian salami.
Éste es un salame italiano.

salt   la sal

There is salt on the table.
Hay sal en la mesa.

same   mismo

The twins always wear the same colors.
Los gemelos llevan siempre los mismos colores.

a b c d e f g h i j k l m n o p q r s t u v w x y z

sand *to* scooter

sand — **la arena**

The children are playing in the sand.
Los niños están jugando
en la arena.

sandal — **la sandalia**

Where is the other sandal?
¿Dónde está la
otra sandalia?

sandwich — **el sándwich**

a cheese sandwich
un sándwich
de queso

saucer — **el platito**

a cup and saucer
una taza y un platito

sausage — **la salchicha**

There are meat sausages and
vegetarian sausages.

Hay
salchichas
de carne y
salchichas
vegetarianas.

save (from danger) **salvar,**
(time or money) **ahorrar**

Mr. Sparks has saved the cat.
El señor Sparks ha
salvado al gato.

Jack is saving
money in this bank.
Jack ahorra dinero
en esta alcancía.

saw — **el serrucho**

I have a saw for cutting wood.

Tengo un serrucho para cortar
madera.

say — **decir**

Yvonne is saying "Sleep
well, my
darling."

Duerme bien,
cariño mío.

Yvonne dice:
"Duerme bien,
cariño mío."

scarf — **la bufanda**

I've made this scarf.
He hecho esta
bufanda.

school — **la escuela,**
el colegio

There are lots of
children at this
school.

Hay muchos niños
en esta escuela.

scissors — **las tijeras**

These are safety scissors.
Éstas son
tijeras de
seguridad.

scooter — **el monopatín,**
(with motor) **la moto**

Shaun has
a green
scooter.

Shaun
tiene un
monopatín
verde.

a b c d e f g h i j k l m n o p q r s t u v w x y z

67

sea — **el mar**

The sea is calm today.

El mar está en calma hoy.

seal — **la foca**

Seals live by the sea.
Las focas viven a
la orilla del mar.

search — **buscar**

They are searching for their friend.
Están buscando a su amigo.

seat — **el asiento**

There are three seats free.

Hay tres asientos libres.

secret — **el secreto**

Amy is telling
Anna a secret.
Amy está
contando
un secreto
a Anna.

see — **ver**

Annie can't
see the clown.
Annie no ve
al payaso.

I'm going to
see my grandparents.
Voy a ver a mis abuelos.

sell — **vender**

Mrs. Hussain is selling
Ethan an apple.
La señora
Hussain vende
una manzana
a Ethan.

send — **enviar**

Jack is sending a letter
to his friend.
Jack envía
una carta
a su amigo.

sentence — **la frase**

This is a complete sentence.

My dad plays tennis.
Mi papá juega al tenis.

Ésta es una frase completa.

sew — **coser**

Robert is sewing his shirt.
Robert está
cosiendo
su camisa.

shadow — **la sombra**

Look at Robert's shadow!
¡Mira la sombra de Robert!

shake — **sacudir**

Anton likes shaking his rattle.
A Anton le gusta
sacudir su
sonajero.

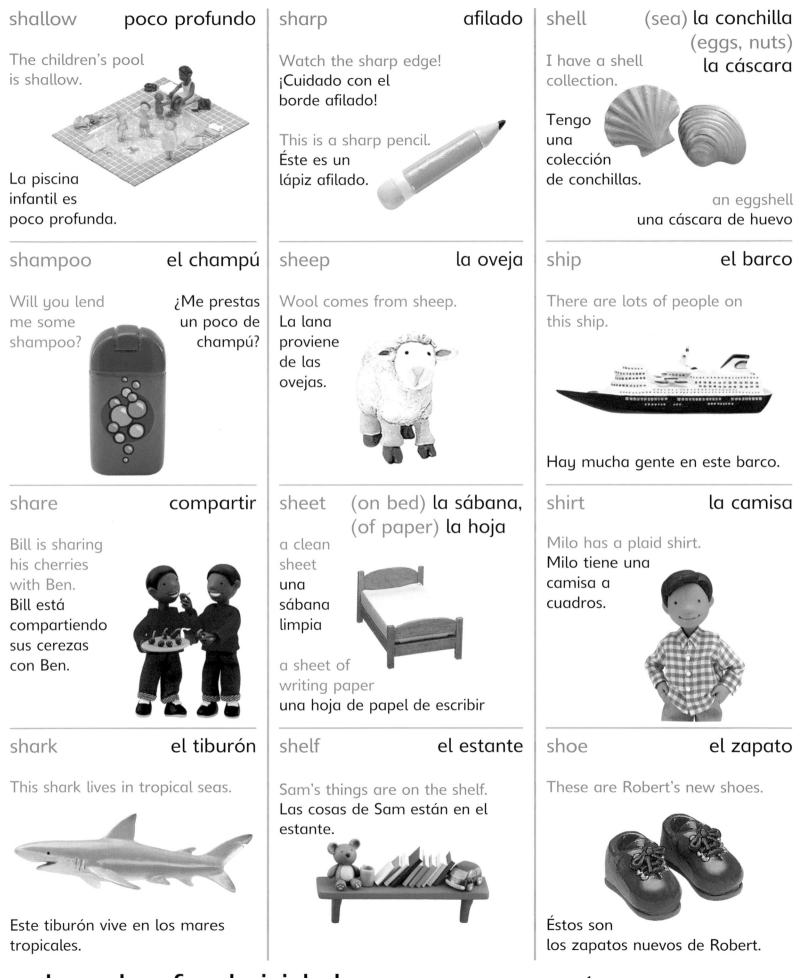

shallow — poco profundo

The children's pool is shallow.

La piscina infantil es poco profunda.

shampoo — el champú

Will you lend me some shampoo?

¿Me prestas un poco de champú?

share — compartir

Bill is sharing his cherries with Ben.
Bill está compartiendo sus cerezas con Ben.

shark — el tiburón

This shark lives in tropical seas.

Este tiburón vive en los mares tropicales.

sharp — afilado

Watch the sharp edge!
¡Cuidado con el borde afilado!

This is a sharp pencil.
Éste es un lápiz afilado.

sheep — la oveja

Wool comes from sheep.
La lana proviene de las ovejas.

sheet — (on bed) la sábana, (of paper) la hoja

a clean sheet
una sábana limpia

a sheet of writing paper
una hoja de papel de escribir

shelf — el estante

Sam's things are on the shelf.
Las cosas de Sam están en el estante.

shell — (sea) la conchilla (eggs, nuts) la cáscara

I have a shell collection.

Tengo una colección de conchillas.

an eggshell
una cáscara de huevo

ship — el barco

There are lots of people on this ship.

Hay mucha gente en este barco.

shirt — la camisa

Milo has a plaid shirt.
Milo tiene una camisa a cuadros.

shoe — el zapato

These are Robert's new shoes.

Éstos son los zapatos nuevos de Robert.

a b c d e f g h i j k l m n o p q r s t u v w x y z

short — corto

Maisie has short hair.
Maisie tiene el pelo corto.

show — mostrar

Jack is showing Thomas his hands.
Jack le está mostrando sus manos a Thomas.

Show me what to do.
Muéstrame lo que hay que hacer.

side — (edge, face) el lado, (team) el equipo

I write on both sides of the paper.
Escribo en ambos lados del papel.

He's on the other side.
Está en el equipo contrario.

shorts — el pantalón corto

brightly colored shorts
un pantalón corto de colores fuertes

shower — (to wash) la ducha, (rain) el aguacero

Robert is taking a shower.
Robert se da una ducha.

sun and showers
sol y aguacero

sign¹ — (road) la señal, (symbol) el símbolo

This sign means "no buses".
Esta señal quiere decir "No autobuses".

@ is the sign for "at".
@ es el símbolo para "a".

shoulder — el hombro

This is Jack's shoulder.
Ésta es el hombro de Jack.

shrink — encogerse

Wool clothes sometimes shrink in hot water.
La ropa de lana se encoge a veces en el agua caliente.

sign² — firmar

The paper says "Sign here please".

Firma aquí por favor

shout — gritar

¡PÁRATE, PIP!

Jack is shouting, "Stop, Pip!"
Jack está gritando "¡Párate, Pip!"

shut — cerrar

Danny is shutting the door.
Danny está cerrando la puerta.

since — desde

PLAZA MAYOR
22

They've been waiting since noon.
Están esperando desde el mediodía.

a b c d e f g h i j k l m n o p q r s t u v w x y z

sing — cantar

Molly can sing very well.
Molly canta muy bien.

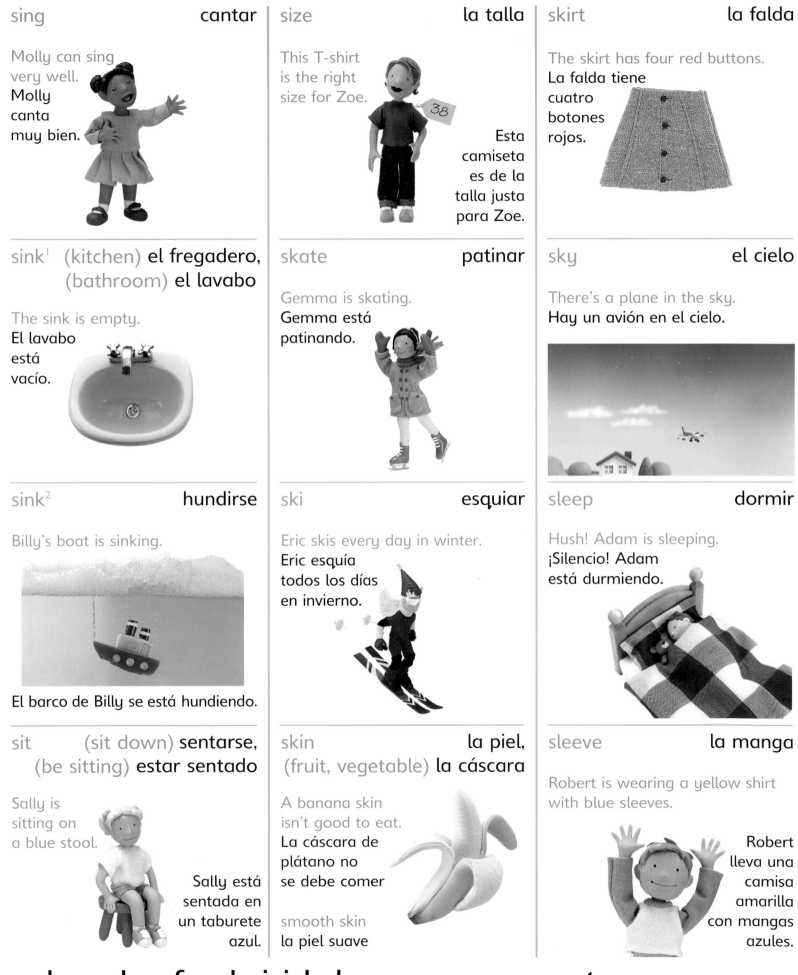

sink¹ (kitchen) el fregadero, (bathroom) el lavabo

The sink is empty.
El lavabo está vacío.

sink² — hundirse

Billy's boat is sinking.
El barco de Billy se está hundiendo.

sit (sit down) sentarse, (be sitting) estar sentado

Sally is sitting on a blue stool.
Sally está sentada en un taburete azul.

size — la talla

This T-shirt is the right size for Zoe.
Esta camiseta es de la talla justa para Zoe.

38

skate — patinar

Gemma is skating.
Gemma está patinando.

ski — esquiar

Eric skis every day in winter.
Eric esquía todos los días en invierno.

skin — la piel, (fruit, vegetable) la cáscara

A banana skin isn't good to eat.
La cáscara de plátano no se debe comer

smooth skin
la piel suave

skirt — la falda

The skirt has four red buttons.
La falda tiene cuatro botones rojos.

sky — el cielo

There's a plane in the sky.
Hay un avión en el cielo.

sleep — dormir

Hush! Adam is sleeping.
¡Silencio! Adam está durmiendo.

sleeve — la manga

Robert is wearing a yellow shirt with blue sleeves.
Robert lleva una camisa amarilla con mangas azules.

a b c d e f g h i j k l m n o p q r s t u v w x y z

slice (cake) **la porción,** (meat, cheese) **la rodaja**

a slice of cake
una porción de pastel

a slice of salami
una rodaja de salame

slipper **la zapatilla**

Polly has pink, bunny-shaped slippers.
Polly tiene unas zapatillas color rosa en forma de conejo.

small **chico, pequeño**

Leila is a small girl.
Leila es una niña chica.

slide¹ **el tobogán**

Sacha and Suki love going on the slide.
A Sacha y a Suki les encanta bajar por el tobogán.

slow **lento**

This is a slow, old train.
Éste es un tren viejo y lento.

smell **oler**

Let me smell the flowers.
Déjame oler las flores.

This cat smells bad.
Este gato huele mal.

slide² **deslizarse**

Denise is sliding down first.
Denise se desliza primero.

slowly **despacio**

Please speak more slowly!
¡Hable más despacio por favor!

Sally is going slowly.
Sally va despacio.

smile **sonreír**

Jack is smiling.
Jack está sonriendo.

slip **resbalarse**

Anna has slipped on the banana skin.
Anna se ha resbalado en la cáscara de plátano.

slug **la babosa**

There are slugs in the garden.
Hay babosas en el jardín.

smooth (to touch) **suave,** (level) **plano**

Babies have smooth skin.
Los bebés tienen la piel suave.

The road is smooth here.
La carretera está plana acá.

snail *to* soon

snail   **el caracol**

A snail is like a slug with a little house.

El caracol es como una babosa con una casita.

soccer   **el fútbol**

Neil plays soccer every Saturday.
Neil juega al fútbol todos los sábados.

soil   **la tierra**

It's good soil for my plant.
Es buena tierra para mi planta.

snake   **la serpiente**

There's a snake in the tree.
Hay una serpiente en el árbol.

sock   **el calcetín**

Luke has striped socks.
Luke lleva unos calcetines a rayas.

soldier   **el soldado**

Tony is dressed up as a soldier.
Tony está disfrazado de soldado.

snow   **la nieve, (to snow) nevar**

They're playing in the snow.
Están jugando en la nieve.

sofa   **el sofá**

Alexa is reading on the sofa.
Alexa está leyendo en el sofá.

song   **la canción**

boom ba ba, boom ba ba

Natalie is singing a song.
Natalie canta una canción.

soap   **el jabón**

My soap is pink.
Mi jabón es rosa.

soft   **suave**

The white kitten has soft fur.
El gatito blanco tiene la piel suave.

soon   **pronto**

It will soon be two o'clock.

Pronto serán las dos.

a b c d e f g h i j k l m n o p q r **s** t u v w x y z

sort   la clase, el tipo

different sorts of food
varios tipos de comida

sound   el ruido

¡Hola!

That funny
sound is the parrot.
**Ese ruido tan raro
lo hace el loro.**

soup   la sopa

a can of vegetable soup
**una lata de
sopa de
verduras**

space   (place) el lugar,
(room *or* stars) el espacio

There are two free spaces.
Hay dos lugares libres.

Astronauts travel into space.
Los astronautas viajan al espacio.

spacecraft   la nave espacial

A rocket
is a spacecraft.
**Un cohete es
una nave espacial.**

speak   hablar

Mrs. Rose is speaking to her
friend.

¡Hola!

¿Qué tal?

**La señora
Rose habla
con su amiga.**

special   especial

a special day
un día especial

Electricians need
special tools
**Los electricistas
necesitan
herramientas
especiales.**

spell¹   el hechizo

a witch's spell
**un hechizo
de bruja**

spell²   deletrear

Oliver can spell his first name
**Oliver sabe
deletrear
su nombre.**

OLIVER

spend   (money) gastar,
(time) pasar

Danny spends
his money
on toys.
**Danny gasta
la paga en
juguetes.**

spider   la araña

Maddy hates
spiders,
but I don't
mind them.

**Maddy
odia a
las arañas,
pero a mí no me molestan.**

spill   derramar

The cat has spilled the mustard.

**El gato ha
derramado
la mostaza.**

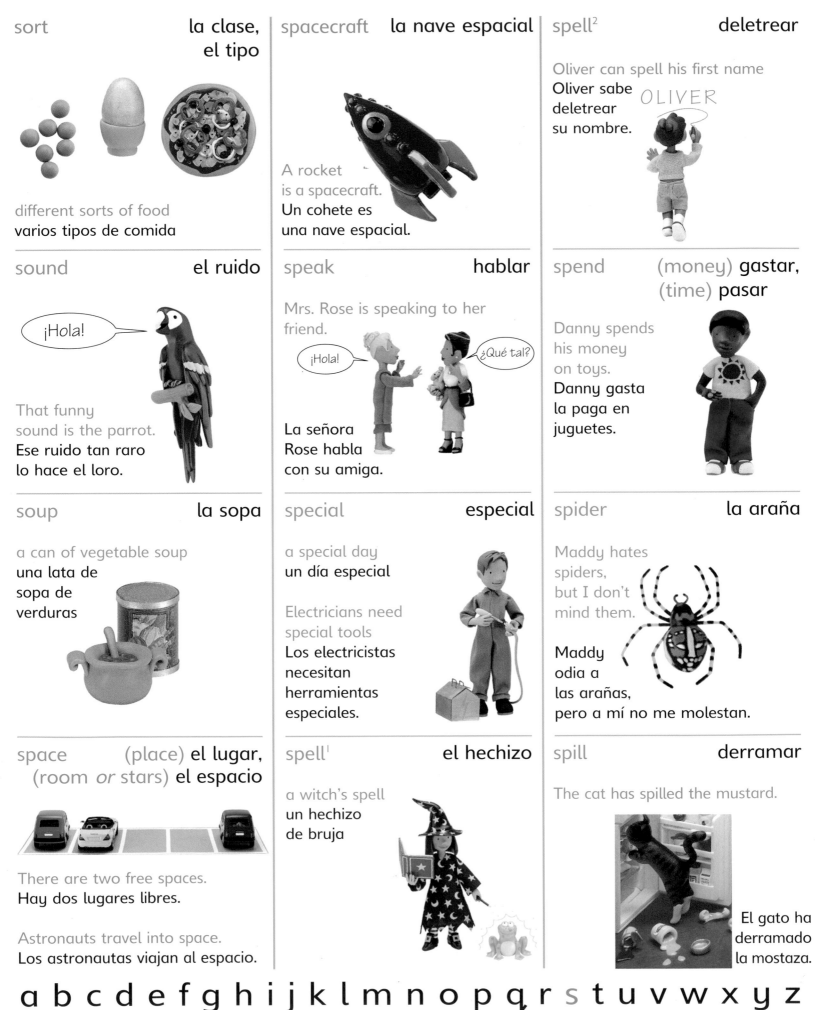

a b c d e f g h i j k l m n o p q r s t u v w x y z

spinach — las espinacas

Spinach is a leafy vegetable.

Las espinacas son verduras con muchas hojas.

splash — salpicar

Polly is splashing water everywhere.

Polly salpica agua por todas partes.

sponge — la esponja

a bath sponge
una esponja de baño

spoon — la cuchara

I need a spoon to eat my soup.
Necesito una cuchara para tomar la sopa.

sports — el deporte

They all enjoy doing sports.

A todos les gusta hacer deporte.

spot[1] — la mancha

This dog has black spots.

Este perro tiene manchas negras.

I have a spot on my shirt.
Tengo una mancha en la camisa.

spot[2] — descubrir

I've spotted a clown.
He descubierto un payaso.

squirrel — la ardilla

There are red squirrels and gray squirrels.

Hay ardillas rojas y ardillas grises.

stairs — la escalera

There's red carpet on the stairs.
Hay una alfombra roja en la escalera.

stamp — la estampilla, el timbre

This letter has a stamp.
Esta carta lleva una estampilla.

Oliver Comelotodo
C/ Desayuno 4, 3°
51000 Merienda

stand (stand up) levantarse, (be standing) estar de pie

Alex is standing.
Alex está de pie.

star — la estrella

The stars are shining.
Las estrellas están brillando.

Natalie, the singer, is a big star.
Natalie, la cantante, es una gran estrella.

a b c d e f g h i j k l m n o p q r **s** t u v w x y z

start   **empezar**

The birds are starting to eat the seeds.

Los pájaros empiezan a comer las semillas.

stick¹   el palo, (twig) **la ramita**

a stick for my dog

un palo para mi perro

sting   **picar**

Amy is afraid that the bee will sting her.

Amy tiene miedo de que la abeja le pique.

station   **la estación**

There are two trains in the station.

Hay dos trenes en la estación.

stick²   **pegar**

Polly is sticking her drawing to the wall.

Polly está pegando su dibujo en la pared.

stir   **revolver**

Jack is stirring the mixture.

Jack está revolviendo la mezcla.

stay   **quedarse,** (visit) **alojarse**

The cows stay in the field.

Las vacas se quedan en el campo.

He's staying at our house.
Se aloja en nuestra casa.

still¹   (calm) **quieto,** (not moving at all) **inmóvil**

Milo is staying still.
Milo se queda quieto.

The car is standing still.
El coche está inmóvil.

stone   **la piedra**

stones from the garden

unas piedras del jardín

steep   **empinado**

It's a steep path.
Es un sendero empinado.

still²   **todavía**

Oliver's still hungry.
Oliver todavía tiene hambre.

He still has some apples left.
Todavía le quedan manzanas.

stool   **el taburete**

a small, blue stool
un pequeño taburete azul

a b c d e f g h i j k l m n o p q r **s** t u v w x y z

stop parar, (yourself) pararse

Jan is stopping at the gate.
Jan se para ante la barrera.

The police are stopping the cars.
La policía está parando a los coches.

storm la tempestad

a storm at sea
una tempestad en el mar

story el cuento

Polly is writing a story.
Polly está escribiendo un cuento.

El anillo mágico
❧
por Polly Dot

Había una vez una bellísima princesa que vivía en un magnífico castillo rodeado de un bosque encantado. Un día, la princesa

straight (line) recto, (hair) liso

a straight path
un sendero recto

Leslie has straight hair.
Leslie tiene el pelo liso.

strawberry la fresa

Strawberries are my favorite fruit.
Las fresas son mi fruta preferida.

street la calle

There are stores on this street.
En esta calle hay tiendas.

string la cuerda

Can you lend me some string?
¿Me prestas un poco de cuerda?

strong fuerte, (solid) sólido

a strong man
un hombre fuerte

strong coffee
café fuerte

The stool isn't very strong.
El taburete no es muy sólido.

study[1] el estudio

Mom's study el estudio de mamá

study[2] estudiar

Sara is studying the Romans.
Sara está estudiando los Romanos.

suddenly de repente

Suddenly Asha drops the vase.
De repente, Asha deja caer el florero.

sugar el azúcar

I need sugar to make a cake.
Necesito azúcar para hacer un pastel.

a b c d e f g h i j k l m n o p q r s t u v w x y z

suitcase — la maleta

This is Mr. Brand's suitcase.
Ésta es la maleta del señor Brand.

sunglasses — las gafas de sol

Polly has pink sunglasses with blue flowers.

Polly tiene unas gafas de sol color rosa con flores azules.

swan — el cisne

There's a swan on the river.

Hay un cisne en el río.

sum — la suma

I can do these sums.
Sé hacer estas sumas.

$$8 + 2 =$$
$$4 - 2 =$$
$$10 \times 4 =$$

supermarket — el supermercado

Dad is at the supermarket.
Papa está en el super-mercado.

sweep — barrer

Anna is sweeping the kitchen.
Anna está barriendo la cocina.

sun — el sol

The sun is shining today.
Hoy brilla el sol.

sure — seguro

Dad is sure they've bought everything.
Papá está seguro de que han comprado todo.

sweet — (taste) dulce, (cute) gracioso

The cake is very sweet.
El pastel está muy dulce.

This kitten is very sweet.
Este gatito es muy gracioso.

sunflower — el girasol

Aggie has some nice sunflowers.
Aggie tiene unos girasoles bonitos.

surprise — la sorpresa

What a surprise!
¡Qué sorpresa! ¡BÚU!

swim — nadar

Pete can swim very well.
Pete nada muy bien.

a b c d e f g h i j k l m n o p q r **s** t u v w x y z

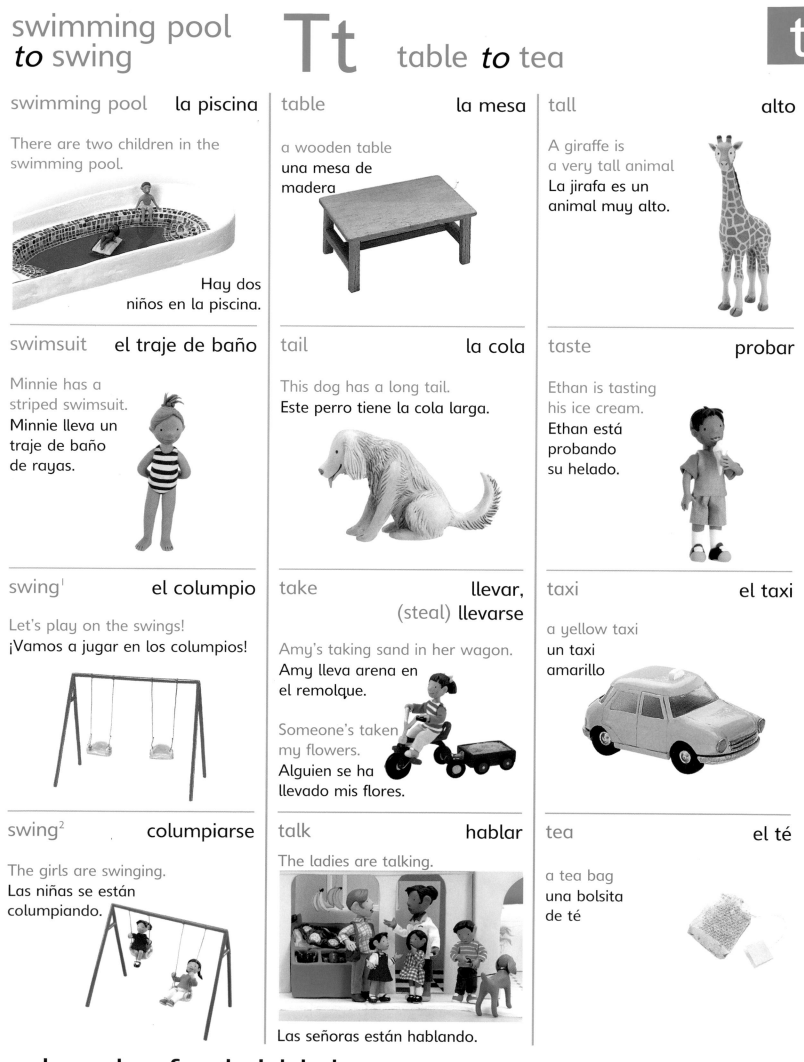

swimming pool   **la piscina**

There are two children in the swimming pool.

Hay dos niños en la piscina.

swimsuit   **el traje de baño**

Minnie has a striped swimsuit.
Minnie lleva un traje de baño de rayas.

swing¹   **el columpio**

Let's play on the swings!
¡Vamos a jugar en los columpios!

swing²   **columpiarse**

The girls are swinging.
Las niñas se están columpiando.

table   **la mesa**

a wooden table
una mesa de madera

tail   **la cola**

This dog has a long tail.
Este perro tiene la cola larga.

take   **llevar, (steal) llevarse**

Amy's taking sand in her wagon.
Amy lleva arena en el remolque.

Someone's taken my flowers.
Alguien se ha llevado mis flores.

talk   **hablar**

The ladies are talking.

Las señoras están hablando.

tall   **alto**

A giraffe is a very tall animal
La jirafa es un animal muy alto.

taste   **probar**

Ethan is tasting his ice cream.
Ethan está probando su helado.

taxi   **el taxi**

a yellow taxi
un taxi amarillo

tea   **el té**

a tea bag
una bolsita de té

a b c d e f g h i j k l m n o p q r s t u v w x y z

teacher — el maestro, la maestra, el profesor, la profesora*

3 x 3 =

Our teacher is Mr. Levy.
Nuestro maestro es el señor Levy.

team — el equipo

This is Neil's team.
Éste es el equipo de Neil.

teddy bear — el osito

This teddy bear has a red scarf.
Este osito lleva una bufanda roja.

telephone — el teléfono

Where is the telephone, please?
¿Dónde está el teléfono, por favor?

television — la televisión

There's nothing on television this evening.
No hay nada en la televisión esta tarde.

tell — (explain) contar, (give instruction) decir

Mrs. Beef is telling them the story.
La señora Beef les cuenta la historia.

Tell Dad to call me.
Dí a papá que me llame.

tent — la tienda

Jack has a little, yellow tent.
Jack tiene una pequeña tienda amarilla.

thank — dar las gracias

Polly is thanking Marco for her present.
Polly está dando las gracias a Marco por su regalo.

Muchas gracias

thin — (line) fino, (person, animal) delgado

thin string
cuerda fina

a thin cat
un gato delgado

thing — la cosa

Tina still has some things to do.
Tina todavía tiene cosas que hacer.

think — (believe) creer, (consider) pensar

I think he is ready.
Creo que está listo.

Maddy thinks spiders are horrible
Maddy piensa que las arañas son horribles.

(to be) thirsty — tener sed

Polly is very thirsty.
Polly tiene mucha sed.

a b c d e f g h i j k l m n o p q r s t u v w x y z

* In Mexico, a *maestro* or *maestra* teaches children aged 12 and above; a *profesor* or *profesora* teaches younger children. In other Spanish-speaking countries, it is the other way around.

through *to* toe

through   por, a través

Mr. Bun is going out through the front door.
El señor Bun sale por la puerta de entrada.

throw   echar, tirar

Anna is throwing the ball to Jack.
Anna tira la pelota a Jack.

thumb   el pulgar

This is Polly's thumb.
Éste es el pulgar de Polly.

ticket   el boleto

I've already bought my ticket.
Ya he comprado mi boleto.

tie   atar

Someone has tied the ribbons.
Alguien ha atado las cintas.

tiger   el tigre

Tigers live in Asia.
Los tigres viven en Asia.

time   (on a clock) la hora, (time taken) el tiempo

What time is it?
¿Qué hora es?

The journey doesn't take much time.
El viaje no toma mucho tiempo.

tiny   minúsculo

a small cat and a tiny cat

un gato pequeño y un gato minúsculo

tip   la punta

The tip of the fox's tail is white.

La punta de la cola del zorro es blanca.

toast   el pan tostado

The toast is ready.
El pan tostado está listo.

toddler   el niño pequeño

Joshua is still a toddler.
Joshua todavía es un niño pequeño.

toe   el dedo del pie

Toes are at the end of feet.
Los dedos del pie están en la punta de los pies.

a b c d e f g h i j k l m n o p q r s t u v w x y z

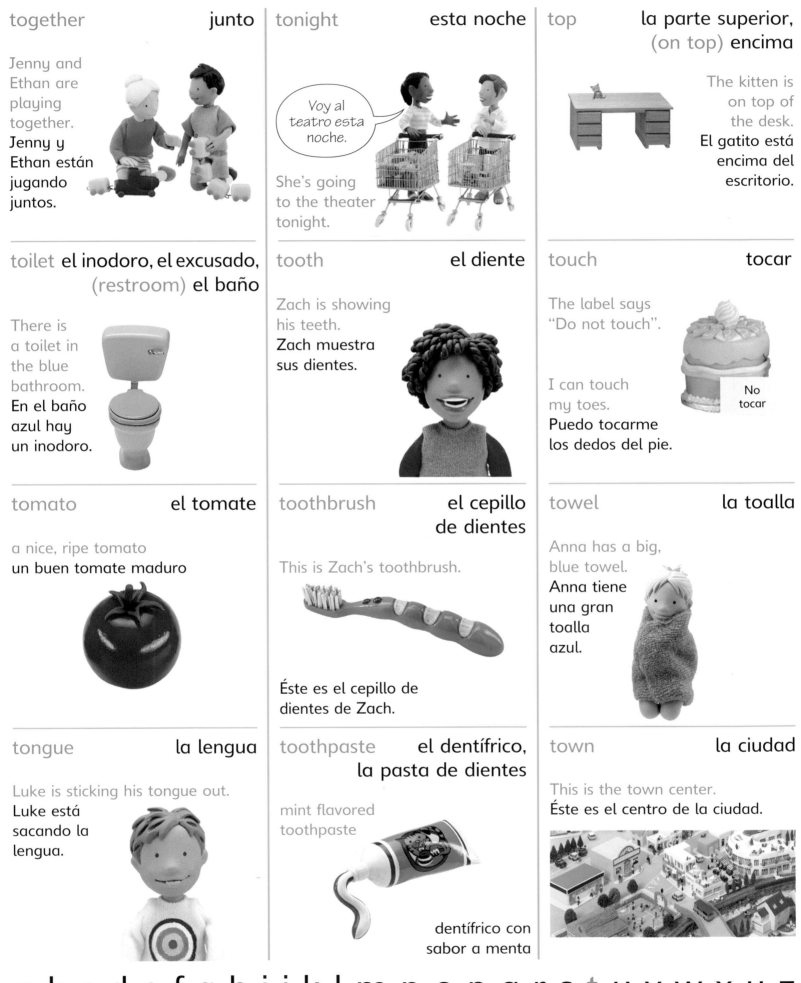

together — junto

Jenny and Ethan are playing together.
Jenny y Ethan están jugando juntos.

tonight — esta noche

Voy al teatro esta noche.

She's going to the theater tonight.

top — la parte superior, (on top) encima

The kitten is on top of the desk.
El gatito está encima del escritorio.

toilet el inodoro, el excusado, (restroom) el baño

There is a toilet in the blue bathroom.
En el baño azul hay un inodoro.

tooth — el diente

Zach is showing his teeth.
Zach muestra sus dientes.

touch — tocar

The label says "Do not touch".

I can touch my toes.
Puedo tocarme los dedos del pie.

No tocar

tomato — el tomate

a nice, ripe tomato
un buen tomate maduro

toothbrush — el cepillo de dientes

This is Zach's toothbrush.

Éste es el cepillo de dientes de Zach.

towel — la toalla

Anna has a big, blue towel.
Anna tiene una gran toalla azul.

tongue — la lengua

Luke is sticking his tongue out.
Luke está sacando la lengua.

toothpaste — el dentífrico, la pasta de dientes

mint flavored toothpaste

dentífrico con sabor a menta

town — la ciudad

This is the town center.
Éste es el centro de la ciudad.

a b c d e f g h i j k l m n o p q r s t u v w x y z

toy — **el juguete**

Joshua has lots of toys.

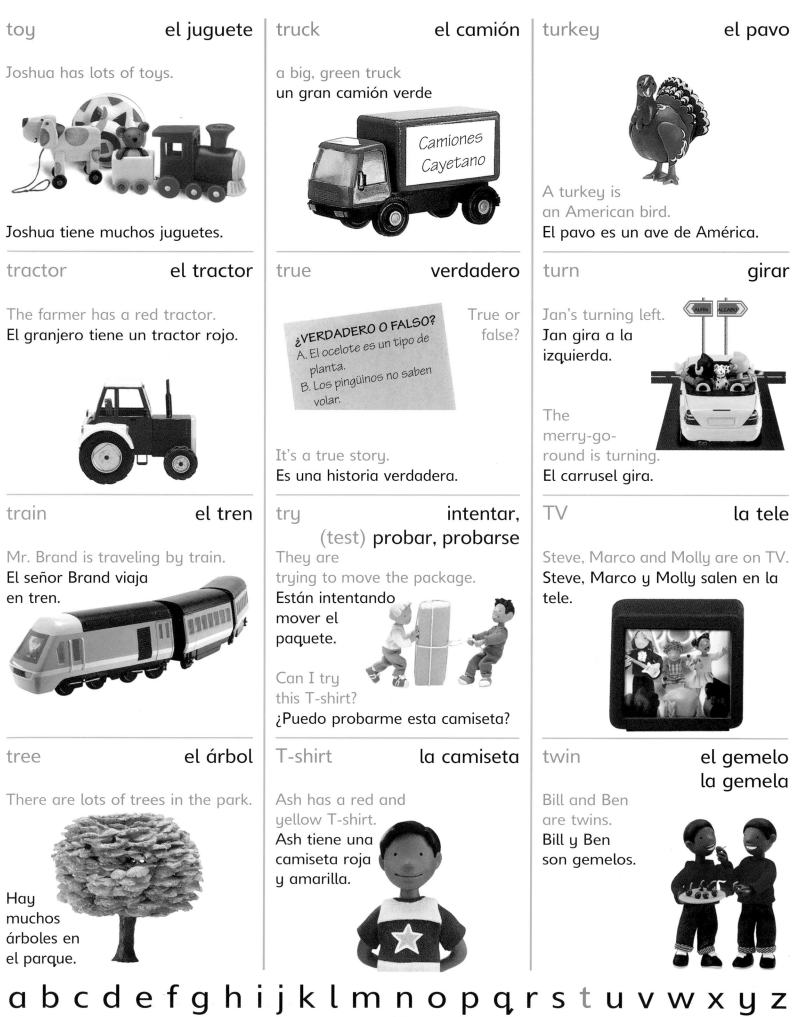

Joshua tiene muchos juguetes.

tractor — **el tractor**

The farmer has a red tractor.
El granjero tiene un tractor rojo.

train — **el tren**

Mr. Brand is traveling by train.
El señor Brand viaja en tren.

tree — **el árbol**

There are lots of trees in the park.

Hay muchos árboles en el parque.

truck — **el camión**

a big, green truck
un gran camión verde

Camiones Cayetano

true — **verdadero**

True or false?

¿VERDADERO O FALSO?
A. El ocelote es un tipo de planta.
B. Los pingüinos no saben volar.

It's a true story.
Es una historia verdadera.

try — **intentar, (test) probar, probarse**

They are trying to move the package.
Están intentando mover el paquete.

Can I try this T-shirt?
¿Puedo probarme esta camiseta?

T-shirt — **la camiseta**

Ash has a red and yellow T-shirt.
Ash tiene una camiseta roja y amarilla.

turkey — **el pavo**

A turkey is an American bird.
El pavo es un ave de América.

turn — **girar**

Jan's turning left.
Jan gira a la izquierda.

The merry-go-round is turning.
El carrusel gira.

TV — **la tele**

Steve, Marco and Molly are on TV.
Steve, Marco y Molly salen en la tele.

twin — **el gemelo la gemela**

Bill and Ben are twins.
Bill y Ben son gemelos.

a b c d e f g h i j k l m n o p q r s t u v w x y z

ugly — feo

This fish is ugly.
Este pez es feo.

undress — desnudarse

Luke is undressing.
Luke se está desnudando.

upside down — al revés

The picture is upside down.
El cuadro está al revés.

umbrella — el paraguas

Robert has a big umbrella.
Robert tiene un gran paraguas.

unhappy — triste

Liddy feels very unhappy.
Liddy se siente muy triste.

use — usar

Mr. Clack is using a saw.
El señor Clack está usando un serrucho.

under — debajo

The kitten is hiding under the boards.

El gatito se esconde debajo de las tablas.

upright — derecho

Tony is standing upright.
Tony está derecho.

useful — útil

A wheelbarrow is useful in the garden.
Una carretilla es útil en el jardín.

understand — entender

I don't understand what Ben is saying.
No entiendo lo que dice Ben.

ta-ta ¡uh!

upset — molesto

Mrs. Beef is upset.
La señora Beef está molesta.

usually — normalmente

Sara usually cycles to school.
Normalmente, Sara va a la escuela en bicicleta.

a b c d e f g h i j k l m n o p q r s t **u** v w x y z

Vv vacuum cleaner *to* voice

vacuum cleaner — la aspiradora

Can you lend me the vacuum cleaner?

¿Me prestas la aspiradora?

vase — el florero

an orange vase with purple flowers

un florero de color naranja con flores moradas.

vegetable — la verdura

different vegetables
varias verduras

very — muy

Flora is dirty and Sally is very dirty.
Flora está sucia y Sally está muy sucia.

view — la vista

a nice view of the country

una bonita vista del campo

visit — visitar

The children are visiting the museum.
Los niños visitan el museo.

visitor — el invitado / la invitada

The visitors are arriving.
Los invitados están llegando.

voice — la voz

Molly has a lovely voice.

¡Laaaaaa!

Molly tiene buena voz.

Ww wait *to* wake — w

wait — esperar

They are waiting for the bus.
Están esperando al autobús.

waiter — el camarero

The waiter is bringing a cup of tea.
El camarero trae un té.

waitress — la camarera

The waitress is bringing two cups of coffee.
La camarera trae dos cafés.

wake (someone) despertar, (wake up) despertarse

Sam is waking up.

Sam se está despertando.

a b c d e f g h i j k l m n o p q r s t u v w x y z

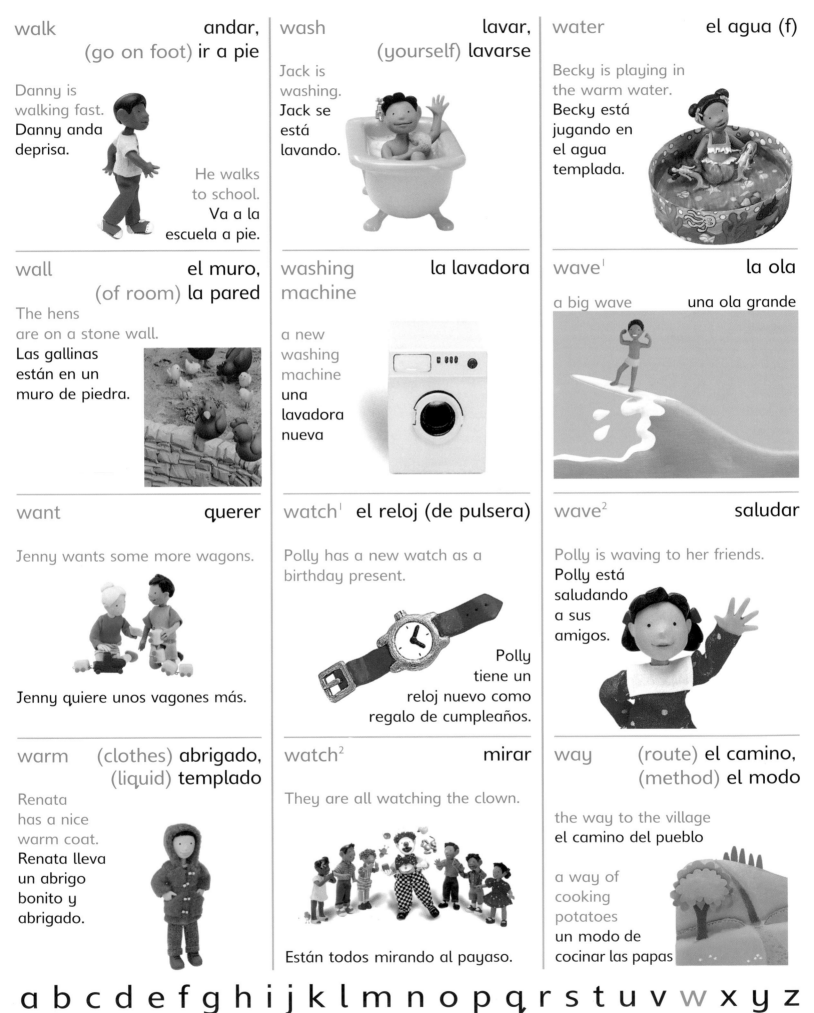

walk — andar, (go on foot) ir a pie

Danny is walking fast.
Danny anda deprisa.

He walks to school.
Va a la escuela a pie.

wall — el muro, (of room) la pared

The hens are on a stone wall.
Las gallinas están en un muro de piedra.

want — querer

Jenny wants some more wagons.

Jenny quiere unos vagones más.

warm — (clothes) abrigado, (liquid) templado

Renata has a nice warm coat.
Renata lleva un abrigo bonito y abrigado.

wash — lavar, (yourself) lavarse

Jack is washing.
Jack se está lavando.

washing machine — la lavadora

a new washing machine
una lavadora nueva

watch¹ — el reloj (de pulsera)

Polly has a new watch as a birthday present.

Polly tiene un reloj nuevo como regalo de cumpleaños.

watch² — mirar

They are all watching the clown.

Están todos mirando al payaso.

water — el agua (f)

Becky is playing in the warm water.
Becky está jugando en el agua templada.

wave¹ — la ola

a big wave — una ola grande

wave² — saludar

Polly is waving to her friends.
Polly está saludando a sus amigos.

way — (route) el camino, (method) el modo

the way to the village
el camino del pueblo

a way of cooking potatoes
un modo de cocinar las papas

a b c d e f g h i j k l m n o p q r s t u v w x y z

wear — llevar

Miriam is wearing a red suit.
Miriam lleva
un traje rojo.

weather — el tiempo

winter weather
tiempo invernal

web (spider's) la telaraña, (World Wide) Web el Web

a spider's web
una telaraña

a Web site
un sitio Web

week — la semana

the days of the week
los días
de la
semana

lunes
martes
miércoles
jueves
viernes
sábado
domingo

well — bien

How are you?
I'm very well,
thank you.
¿Qué tal?
Muy bien, gracias.

Sara reads
very well.
Sara lee muy bien.

wet — mojado, (soaking) empapado

Jem the
plumber
is all wet.
Jem, el
plomero,
se ha
empapado.

whale — la ballena, (killer whale) la orca

Killer whales
swim very
fast.

Las orcas
nadan muy rápido.

wheel — la rueda

a big truck wheel
una gran
rueda de
camión

while — mientras

While his parents are talking,
Jack is eating a cupcake.
Mientras sus
padres charlan,
Jack está
comiendo
un pastel.

wide — ancho

The sofa is quite wide.

El sofá es bastante ancho.

wild — salvaje

wild
animals

unos animales
salvajes

win — ganar

The pink cake has won first prize.
El pastel rosa ha ganado el
primer premio.

a b c d e f g h i j k l m n o p q r s t u v w x y z

wind   el viento

a windy
day
un día
de viento

window   la ventana

Look out of the window.
Mira por la ventana.

wish   el deseo

The fairy can
grant three
wishes.

El hada concede
tres deseos.

witch   la bruja

There are
witches in
fairy tales.
Hay brujas
en los cuentos
de hadas.

with   con

Ben sleeps with his teddy bear.
Ben duerme con su osito.

a bird with blue feet
un pájaro con las
patas azules

woman   la mujer

This woman is
a gardener.
Esta mujer es
jardinera.

wood   la madera,
                 (trees) el bosque

This table is
made of wood.
Esta mesa es
de madera.

There are woods
beside the lake.
Hay bosques
a la orilla del lago.

word   la palabra

a list of words
una lista de
palabras

arriba
brillante
dirección
leer

work   (do a job) **trabajar,**
              (function) **funcionar**

Mick works
all day.
Mick trabaja
todo el día.

This computer
doesn't work.
Esta computadora no funciona.

world   el mundo

all the countries
in the world
todos los
países
del
mundo

write   escribir

Oliver is writing his first name.
Oliver está
escribiendo
su nombre.

OLIVER

wrong   equivocado

the wrong
answers
las respuestas
equivocadas

$2 + 3 = 7$ X
$4 + 6 = 9$ X
$5 - 3 = 4$ X

a b c d e f g h i j k l m n o p q r s t u v w x y z

Xx x *to* xylophone

x   (kiss) **un beso,**
          (in sums) **x**

Love, Olivia xxx
Un beso, Olivia

$$2 \times 2 = 4$$

(two times two equals four)
(dos por dos son cuatro)

Xmas   **Navidad (f)**

Happy Xmas!
¡Feliz
Navidad!

---

x-ray   **los rayos-x,**
(photo) **la radiografía**

The
x-ray shows
Robert's
skeleton.
La radiografía
muestra el
esqueleto
de Robert.

---

xylophone   **el xilófono**

This xylophone has six notes.
Este xilófono tiene seis notas.

Yy yawn *to* young

yawn   **bostezar**

Sam's yawning.
Sam está bostezando.

---

year   **el año**

Flora is five years old. Annie
is a year older.
Flora tiene cinco
años. Annie tiene
un año más.

the days
of the year
los días del año

---

yet   **todavía**

Ben can't
walk yet.

Ben
todavía
no sabe
andar.

---

young   **joven,**
          pequeño

young children
niños pequeños

Zz zebra *to* zoo

z

zebra   **la cebra**

Zebras live in Africa.
Las cebras
viven en
África.

---

zero   **cero**

Five take away five equals zero.
Cinco menos cinco son cero.

$$5 - 5 = 0$$

---

zipper   **la cremallera**

The zipper is half open.
La cremallera
está medio
abierta.

---

zoo   **el jardín zoológico**

There's a panda at the zoo.
Hay un panda en el jardín
zoológico.

a b c d e f g h i j k l m n o p q r s t u v w x y z

Colors

Los colores

white blanco

red rojo

black negro

yellow amarillo

blue azul

purple morado

green verde

pink rosa*

orange naranja*

brown marrón

gray gris

Shapes

Las formas

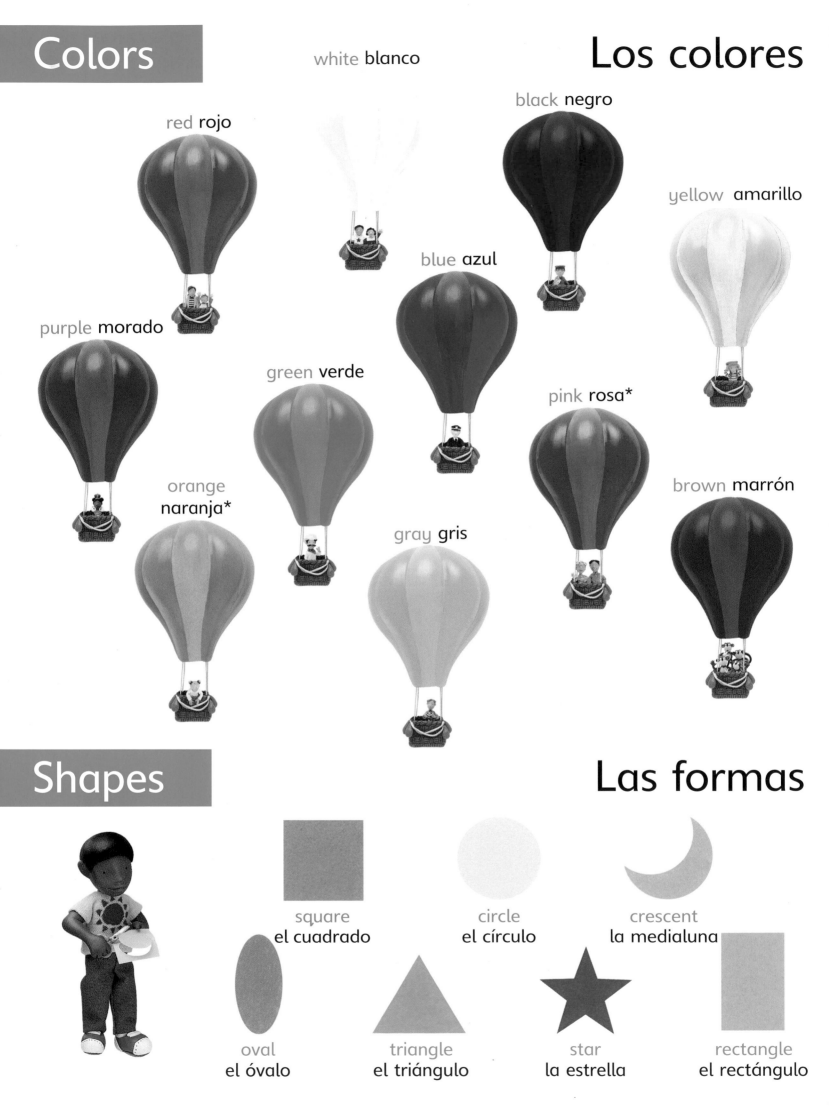

square
el cuadrado

circle
el círculo

crescent
la medialuna

oval
el óvalo

triangle
el triángulo

star
la estrella

rectangle
el rectángulo

* These colors end in –a whether they follow a masculine or a feminine noun.

Numbers

Los números

1st 1º	2nd 2º	3rd 3º	4th 4º	5th 5º	6th 6º	7th 7º	8th 8º	9th 9º	10th 10º
primero	segundo	tercero	cuarto	quinto	sexto	séptimo	octavo	noveno	décimo

1 uno

2 dos

3 tres

4 cuatro

5 cinco

6 seis

7 siete

8 ocho

9 nueve

10 diez

11 once

12 doce

13 trece

14 catorce

15 quince

16 dieciséis

17 diecisiete

18 dieciocho

19 diecinueve

20 veinte

30	40	50	60	70	80	90	100	1000
treinta	cuarenta	cincuenta	sesenta	setenta	ochenta	noventa	cien	mil

Days and months

Los días y los meses

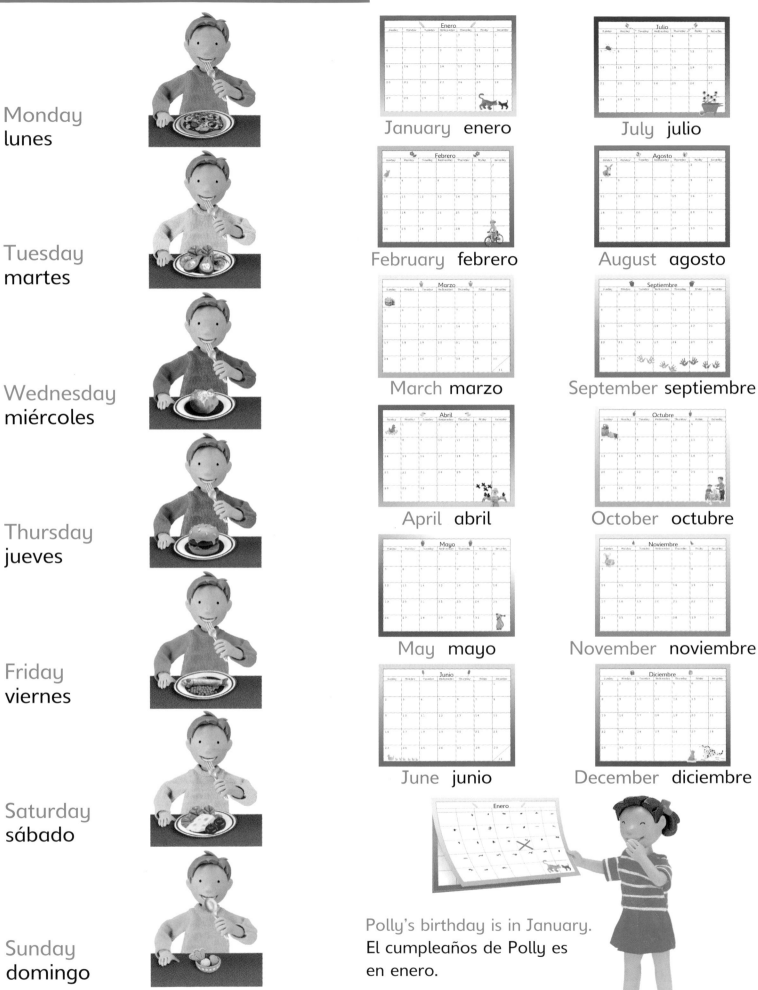

Monday
lunes

Tuesday
martes

Wednesday
miércoles

Thursday
jueves

Friday
viernes

Saturday
sábado

Sunday
domingo

January   enero

February   febrero

March   marzo

April   abril

May   mayo

June   junio

July   julio

August   agosto

September   septiembre

October   octubre

November   noviembre

December   diciembre

Polly's birthday is in January.
El cumpleaños de Polly es
en enero.

Las estaciones

Spring   la primavera

Summer   el verano

Fall   el otoño

Winter   el invierno

Family

La familia

Polly's photo album
el álbum de fotos de Polly

sister, brother
**la hermana,
el hermano**

father
el padre
Dad
Papá

mother
la madre
Mom
Mamá

son
el hijo

daughter
la hija

Dad and his brother
Papá y su hermano

baby
el bebé

grandmother
la abuela
Grandma
Abuela

grandchildren
los nietos

grandfather
el abuelo
Grandpa
Abuelo

aunt
la tía

(girl) cousin
la prima*
uncle
el tío

grandparents
los abuelos

children
los hijos

parents
los padres

* boy cousin would be *el primo*.

Words we use a lot

On these pages you'll find some words that are useful for making sentences, and are used in sentences in the dictionary. Remember that in Spanish some words can change, depending on whether the word that follows is masculine or feminine, singular or plural (see page 3).

about	(story) sobre, (more or less) alrededor de
across	a través
again	otra vez
almost	casi
also	además
always	siempre
and	y
another	otro, otra
any	algún, alguna, algunos, algunas
around	alrededor de
because	porque
but	pero
by	(beside) al lado de, (done by) por
each or every	cada
everybody or everyone	todo el mundo
everything	todo
everywhere	por todas partes
for	para
he	él
her	ella
	(to...) le
	(belonging to...) su, sus
here	acá
him	él
	(to...) le
his	su, sus
I	yo
if	si
in, into	en
it	el, ella, ello

its	su, sus
it's	es, está
just	sólo, solamente
me	mí
	(to...) me
my	mi, mis
myself	yo mismo, mí mismo
no	(not yes) no
	(not one) ni un, ni una
of	de
on	en
or	o
our	nuestro, nuestra, nuestros, nuestras
out of	fuera de
she	ella
so	(so big) tan
	(because of this) así
somebody or someone	alguien
something	algo
sometimes	a veces
somewhere	en algún sitio
than	que
their	su, sus
them	ellos, ellas
	(to...) les
then	entonces
there	allí
there's	hay
they	ellos, ellas
today	hoy
tomorrow	mañana
too	también

unless	a menos que
until	hasta
us	nosotros
	(to...) nos
we	nosotros
what	lo que
	(in questions) qué
which	que
	(in questions) cuál
whose	cuyo
	(in questions) de quién
yes	sí
yesterday	ayer
you	tú, ti or usted or ustedes*
	(to...) te or le or les*
your	tu, tus or su, sus

* You use *tú* for a young person or someone you know very well; *usted* for someone you don't know very well, and *ustedes* for more than one person.

This, that

On page 3, you can see how the word for "the" changes, depending whether a noun is masculine or feminine. The word for "this" is *este*, and it changes in a similar way:

the boy	el chico
this boy	este chico
the word	la palabra
this word	esta palabra

When you are talking about more than one of something (plurals), the word for "these" is *estos* for masculine nouns, and *estas* for feminine ones:

the boys	los chicos
these boys	estos chicos
the words	las palabras
these words	estas palabras

The word for "that" is *ese* if you are talking about something close to the person you are speaking to, and *aquel* if you are talking about something that isn't close. *Eso* and *aquel* change in a similar way to *este*:

Pass me...	Pásame...
... that book	... ese libro
... that cup	... esa taza
... those papers	... esos papeles
... those scissors	... esas tijeras

Look at...	Mira...
... that plane	... aquel avión
... that house	... aquella casa
... those cars	... aquellos coches
... those flowers	... aquellas flores

If *este* or *ese* aren't followed by a noun, they change to *esto* and *eso* (*esta* and *esa* don't change):

Does she need this?	¿Necesita esto?
I don't want that.	No quiero eso.

One, some, all

In Spanish, the words for "one", some" and "all" can change, depending on whether the following noun is masculine or feminine, singular or plural (see page 3). The word for "a" or "an" is the same as the word for "one":

a boy *or* one boy	un chico
a girl *or* one girl	una chica

The word for "some", meaning "several", is *unos* for masculine nouns and *unas* for feminine nouns:

some boys	unos chicos
some girls	unas chicas

The word for "some", meaning "some, not others", is *algunos* for masculine nouns and *algunas* for feminine nouns:

Some boys are wearing shorts.
Algunos chicos llevan pantalones cortos.

Some little girls don't like dolls.
A algunas niñas no les gustan las muñecas.

There isn't a special word for "some" meaning "a little":

I'm eating some bread.
Estoy comiendo pan.

He needs some water.
Necesita agua.

The word for "all" is *todo*, or *toda* in the feminine:

all the time	todo el tiempo
all my life	toda mi vida

When you are talking about more than one, it becomes *todos* for masculine nouns and *todas* for feminine nouns:

all the boys	todos los chicos
all the girls	todas las chicas

Making sentences

To make sentences in Spanish, you usually put the words in the same order as in an English sentence. Remember to make any changes you need for masculine or feminine words in the sentence. Here are some examples from the dictionary:

It's a work of art.
Es una obra de arte.

Patch has found some bones.
Patch ha encontrado unos huesos.

Eric goes very fast on his skis.
Eric va muy rápido en sus esquíes.

Where does the adjective go?

In English, adjectives usually go before the noun they are describing. In Spanish, most adjectives go after the noun:

a healthy breakfast
un desayuno sano

a dangerous snake
una serpiente peligrosa

Becky has green ribbons.
Becky lleva unas cintas verdes.

However, some very common adjectives, such as *bueno*, *grande*, *malo*, can go before the noun. If so, they are shortened to *buen* and *mal* before masculine nouns (only in the singular) or *gran* before all nouns in the singular:

a large amount of pasta
una gran cantidad de pasta

It is possible to have adjectives before and after a noun:

a nice, sweet, green pear
una rica pera verde y dulce

More and most

In English, when you compare things, you often add "er" to an adjective: "A mouse is smaller than a rabbit." Other times, you use "more": "My puzzle is more difficult than yours." In Spanish, you use the word *más* to compare things:

Mountains are higher than hills.
Las montañas son más altas que las colinas.

The car is more expensive than the duck.
El coche es más caro que el pato.

When you compare several things, in English you add "est" to the adjective, or use "most": "This tree's the tallest." "This is the most delicious." In Spanish, you use *el más,* (or *la más* or *los más* or *las más*):

Ben is the youngest.
Ben es el más joven.

These shoes are the most expensive.
Estos zapatos son los más caros.

As in English, you have special words for:

better	mejor
the best	el mejor (la mejor, los mejores, las mejores)
worse	peor
the worst	el peor (la peor, los peores, las peores)

My plane is better than your truck.
Mi avión es mejor que tu camión.

the best in the class
el mejor *or* la mejor de la clase

the worst place to have a picnic
el peor sitio para hacer un picnic

Making questions

To make a question in Spanish, you put the verb before the subject of the sentence, and add question marks at the beginning and end of the sentence. For example:

Is the bus going into town?
¿Va el autobús a la ciudad?

Is the kitten behind the flowerpot?
¿Está el gatito detrás del florero?

You can also make questions beginning with question words, such as:

Who..?	¿Quién..?
Which..?	¿Cuál..? *or* ¿Cuáles?
What..?	¿Qué..?
Where..?	¿Dónde..?
When..?	¿Cuándo..?
Why..?	¿Por qué..?
How..?	¿Cómo..?
How much..?	¿Cuánto..? *or* ¿Cuánta..?
How many..?	¿Cuántos..? *or* ¿Cuántas..?

For example:

What does this word mean?
¿Qué quiere decir esta palabra?

How much do the apples cost?
¿Cuánto cuestan las manzanas?

And there are some other useful words for questions which mostly begin "any–" in English:

anybody *or* anyone	alguien
anything	algo
anywhere	en algún sitio

For example:

Is anybody in the classroom?
¿Hay alguien en el aula?

Does she need anything?
¿Necesita algo?

Have you seen my glasses anywhere?
¿Has visto mis gafas en algún sitio?

Negative sentences

A negative sentence is a "not" sentence, such as "I'm not hungry". To make a sentence negative in Spanish, you just add *no* before the verb:

I'm not hungry.
No tengo hambre.

The bus isn't going into town.
El autobús no va a la ciudad.

The kitten isn't behind the flowerpot.
El gatito no está detrás del florero.

Mom doesn't want cake.
Mamá no quiere pastel.

If there is more than one verb, you only make one negative, as in English:

He doesn't like doing his homework.
No le gusta hacer sus deberes.

Dad hasn't burned the burgers.
Papá no ha quemado las hamburguesas.

There are some useful words for negative sentences which mostly begin "no–" in English (it's the same as saying "not any–"):

nobody *or* no one	nadie
nothing	nada
nowhere	ninguna parte
never	nunca

For example:

There is nobody at home
or There isn't anybody at home.
No hay nadie en casa.

I have nothing to eat
or I don't have anything to eat.
No tengo nada que comer.

This path goes nowhere
or This path doesn't go anywhere.
Este sendero no va a ninguna parte.

The train is never late
or The train isn't ever late.
El tren nunca lleva retraso.

To, from and other useful place words

The Spanish word for "to" (a place or person) is *a*. If it is followed by a masculine noun, it changes to *al*:

They're going to the supermarket.
Van al supermercado.

Jack is sending a letter to his friend.
Jack está enviando una carta a su amigo.

Danny walks to school.
Danny va a la escuela a pie.

Polly is feeding corn to the hens.
Polly está dando maíz a las gallinas.

In Spanish, you often use *a* in places where you wouldn't say "to" in English. Look at some examples from the dictionary:

Alex is calling Pip.
Alex llama a Pip.

Polly and Jack are chasing the dogs.
Polly y Jack persiguen a los perros.

The doctor is taking care of Kirsty.
El médico está cuidando a Kirsty.

This sweater doesn't fit Jenny.
Este suéter no le queda bien a Jenny.

The Spanish word for "at", "in" or "on" is usually *en*:

I've left my bag at home.
He dejado mi bolsa en casa.

Polly and Marco play in a band.
Polly y Marco tocan en una orquesta.

The hens are on a stone wall.
Las gallinas están en un muro de piedra.

Note that when you are talking about where something is, you always use the verb *estar*, even for something that is always there (like a building):

The museum is in the town center.
El museo está en el centro de la ciudad.

The Spanish word for "from", and also "of", is *de*. If it is followed by *el*, you put *de* and *el* together and say *del*:

He's coming from the office.
Viene del despacho.

the bark of a tree
la corteza de un árbol

I'm taking a book from the shelf.
Tomo un libro del estante.

the meaning of the words
el significado de las palabras

De is also part of lots of other useful place expressions:

next to	al lado de
near to	cerca de
a long way from	lejos de
outside	fuera de
inside	dentro de
in front of	delante de
behind	detrás de
opposite	enfrente de
on top of	encima de
underneath	debajo de

For example:

The kitten is next to the flowerpot.
El gatito está al lado del florero.

The store is near the swimming pool.
La tienda está cerca de la piscina.

The house is a long way from the school.
La casa está lejos de la escuela.

The monkey is outside the box.
El mono está fuera de la caja.

The church is opposite the hospital.
La iglesia está enfrente del hospital
(you can also say) frente al hospital.

The kitten is on top of the desk.
El gatito está encima del escritorio.

Verbs

These pages list the verbs (or "doing" words) that appear in the main part of the dictionary. Page 4 explains a little about verbs in Spanish, and how the endings change for "I", "you", "he *or* she", and so on. It also introduces the two Spanish verbs for "to be", *ser* and *estar*.

In this list, you can find the infinitive (the "to" form) and the "–ing" form of the verb, which ends *–ndo* in Spanish. You can also find the "I" and the "he *or* she" form in the present (the form you use to talk about things happening now). To make the "they" form, you add *–n* to the end of the "he *or* she" form. For example:

to speak	hablar
speaking	hablando
I speak	hablo
he speaks *or*	
she speaks	habla
they speak	hablan

These are probably the forms you will find most useful to begin with.

*Reflexive verbs

The verbs marked with an asterisk (*) are a type of verb called a "reflexive verb". They are often used where you would use "... myself", "... yourself", and so on, in English. The main part of the verb works like other verbs, but you also need to put *me*, *te*, *se* and so on, depending on who is doing the action. For example, *lavarse* ("to wash yourself") is formed like this (find out about the different "you" forms on page 4):

I wash myself	me lavo
you wash yourself	te lavas
you wash yourself	(usted) se lava
he washes himself *or*	
she washes herself	se lava
we wash ourselves	nos lavamos
you wash yourselves	(ustedes) se lavan
they wash themselves	se lavan

You also need to say *me*, *te*, *se* and so on when you use the "–ing" form:

I am washing myself Me estoy lavando

abrazar abrazando abrazo abraza	to hug	adivinar adivinando adivino adivina	to guess	andar andando ando anda	to walk	arreglar arreglando arreglo arregla	to fix, to mend
abrir abriendo abro abre	to open	agarrar agarrando agarro agarra	to catch	añadir añadiendo añado añade	to add	arrodillarse* arrodillando me arrodillo se arrodilla	to kneel down
acampar acampando acampo acampa	to camp	ahorrar ahorrando ahorro ahorra	to save (money, time)	apagar apagando apago apaga	to blow out, to put out	asentir (con la abeza) asintiendo asiento asiente	to nod
acordarse* acordando me acuerdo se acuerda	to remember	alcanzar alcanzando alcanzo alcanza	to reach	aprender aprendiendo aprendo aprende	to learn	atar atando ato ata	to tie
acostarse* acostando me acuesto se acuesta	to lie down	alojarse* alojando alojo aloja	to stay (as guest)	apurarse* apurando me apuro se apura	to hurry	ayudar ayudando ayudo ayuda	to help

bailar	to dance	cavar	to dig	congelar	to freeze	coser	to sew
bailando		cavando		congelando	(something)	cosiendo	
bailo		cavo		congelo		coso	
baila		cava		congela		cose	
barrer	to sweep	cerrar	to close,	conocer	to know	crecer	to grow
barriendo		cerrando	to shut	conociendo	(people)	creciendo	
barro		cierro		conozco		crezco	
barre		cierra		conoce		crece	
beber	to drink	cocinar	to cook	conservar	to keep	creer	to think,
bebiendo		cocinando		conservando		creyendo	to believe
bebo		cocino		conservo		creo	
bebe		cocina		conserva		cree	
besar	to kiss	colgar	to hang	construir	to build	cruzar	to cross
besando		colgando		construyendo		cruzando	
beso		cuelgo		construyo		cruzo	
besa		cuelga		construye		cruza	
bostezar	to yawn	columpiarse*	to swing	contar	to tell,	dar	to give
bostezando		columpiando		contando	to count	dando	
bostezo		me columpio		cuento		doy	
bosteza		se columpia		cuenta		da	
buscar	to search	comer	to eat	contestar	to reply	darse* cuenta	to notice,
buscando		comiendo		contestando		dando cuenta	to realize
busco		como		contesto		me doy cuenta	
busca		come		contesta		se da cuenta	
caer	to fall	compartir	to share	copiar	to copy	decir	to say,
cayendo		compartiendo		copiando		diciendo	to tell
caigo		comparto		copio		digo	
cae		comparte		copia		dice	
calentar	to heat	comprar	to buy	correr	to run	dejar	to let,
calentando		comprando		corriendo		dejando	to leave
caliento		compro		corro		dejo	(something)
calienta		compra		corre		deja	
cantar	to sing	conducir	to lead	cortar	to cut	deletrear	to spell
cantando		conduciendo	(direction)	cortando		deletreando	
canto		conduzco		corto		deletreo	
canta		conduce		corta		deletrea	

Gustar, encantar and others

The verbs marked with two asterisks (**) are described in the dictionary as being "the other way around from English". Instead of saying "I like this book" or "I like strawberries", it is as though you were saying "This book pleases me" or "strawberries please me". So if the verb changes, it depends on "book" (singular) or "strawberries" (plural), and not on "I" or "me".

I like this book	me gusta este libro
I like strawberries	me gustan las fresas

If you are talking about another person or other people, you usually put *a* before their name, at the beginning of the sentence:

Beth loves bathing.
A Beth le encanta bañarse.

Becky likes strawberries.
A Becky le gusta las fresas.

My parents don't mind the mess.
A mis padres no les molesta el desorden.

The children love magic tricks.
A los niños les encantan los trucos de magia.

Verbs

derramar — to spill
derramando
derramo
derrama

desaparecer — to disappear
desapareciendo
desaparezco
desaparece

descubrir — to spot
descubriendo
descubro
descubre

deslizarse* — to slide
deslizando
me deslizo
se desliza

desnudarse* — to undress
desnudando
me desnudo
se desnuda

despertarse* — to wake up
despertando
me despierto
se despierta

dibujar — to draw
dibujando
dibujo
dibuja

divertirse* — to enjoy yourself
divirtiendo
me divierto
se divierte

doler — to hurt
doliendo
(no I form)
duele

dormir — to sleep
durmiendo
duermo
duerme

echar — to throw
echando
echo
echa

elegir — to choose, to pick
eligiendo
elijo
elige

empezar — to begin
empezando
empiezo
empieza

empujar — to push
empujando
empujo
empuja

encantar** — to love
encantando
me encanta,
   me encantan
le encanta, le encantan

encogerse* — to shrink
encogiendo
me encojo
se encoge

encontrar — to find
encontrando
encuentro
encuentra

entender — to understand
entendiendo
entiendo
entiende

enviar — to send
enviando
envío
envía

escaparse* — to escape
escapando
me escapo
se escapa

esconder — to hide
escondiendo
escondo
esconde

escribir — to write
escribiendo
escribo
escribe

esperar — to wait, to hope
esperando
espero
espera

esquiar — to ski
esquiando
esquío
esquía

estacionar — to park
estacionando
estaciono
estaciona

estrellarse* — to crash
estrellando
me estrello
se estrella

estudiar — to study
estudiando
estudio
estudia

explicar — to explain
explicando
explico
explica

extrañar — to miss
extrañando
extraño
extraña

fijar — to attach
fijando
fijo
fija

fingir — to pretend
fingiendo
finjo
finge

firmar — to sign
firmando
firmo
firma

flotar — to float
flotando
floto
flota

freír — to fry
friendo
frío
fríe

funcionar — to work (machines)
funcionando
funciono
funciona

ganar — to win
ganando
gano
gana

gastar — to spend
gastando
gasto
gasta

gatear — to crawl
gateando
gateo
gatea

girar — to turn
girando
giro
gira

golpear — to hit
golpeando
golpeo
golpea

graznar — to quack
graznando
grazno
grazna

gritar — to shout
gritando
grito
grita

guardar — to keep
guardando
guardo
guarda

gustar** — to like
gustando
me gusta, me gustan
le gusta, le gustan

hablar — to talk, to speak
hablando
hablo
habla

hacer — to do, to make
haciendo
hago
hace

helarse* — to freeze
helando
me hielo
se hiela

hornear — to bake
horneando
horneo
hornea

hundirse* — to sink
hundiendo
me hundo
se hunde

importar — to matter
importando
(no I form)
importa

inclinarse* — to lean
inclinando
me inclino
se inclina

intentar — to try
intentando
intento
intenta

*see Reflexive verbs on page 100.   **see *Gustar, encantar* and others on page 101.

invitar invitando invito invita	to invite	llorar llorando lloro llora	to cry	morirse* muriendo me muero se muere	to die	patear pateando pateo patea	to kick
ir yendo voy va	to go	llover lloviendo (no I form) llueve	to rain	mostrar mostrando muestro muestra	to show	patinar patinando patino patina	to skate
jugar jugando juego juega	to play	manejar manejando manejo maneja	to drive	mover moviendo muevo mueve	to move	pedir pidiendo pido pide	to ask (for something)
ladrar ladrando ladro ladra	to bark	mantenerse* en equilibrio manteniendo ... me mantengo ... se mantiene ...	to balance	nadar nadando nado nada	to swim	pegar pegando pego pega	to stick
lamer lamiendo lamo lame	to lick	matar matando mato mata	to kill	necesitar necesitando necesito necesita	to need	pelearse* peleando me peleo se pelea	to fight
lavar lavando lavo lava	to wash	medir midiendo mido mide	to measure	nevar nevando (no I form) nieva	to snow	pensar pensando pienso piensa	to think, to consider
leer leyendo leo lee	to read	mentir mintiendo miento miente	to lie	odiar odiando odio odia	to hate	perder perdiendo pierdo pierde	to lose, to miss
levantar levantando levanto levanta	to lift	meter metiendo meto mete	to put (inside)	oír oyendo oigo oye	to hear	perseguir persiguiendo persigo persigue	to chase
limpiar limpiando limpio limpia	to clean	mezclar mezclando mezclo mezcla	to mix	oler oliendo huelo huele	to smell	pertenecer perteneciendo pertenezco pertenece	to belong
llamar llamando llamo llama	to call	mirar mirando miro mira	to look, to watch	olvidar olvidando olvido olvida	to forget	pescar pescando pesco pesca	to fish
llegar llegando llego llega	to arrive, to reach	molestar** molestando me molesta, me molestan le molesta, le molestan	to mind	pagar pagando pago paga	to pay	picar picando pico pica	to itch, to sting
llenar llenando lleno llena	to fill	montar (a caballo) montando monto monta	to ride	parar parando paro para	to stop	pintar pintando pinto pinta	to paint
llevar llevando llevo lleva	to carry, to take to wear, to bring	morder mordiendo muerdo muerde	to bite	pasar pasando paso pasa	to pass, to happen, to spend (time)	planear planeando planeo planea	to plan

*see Reflexive verbs on page 100.   **see *Gustar, encantar* and others on page 101.

Verbs

plegar — to fold
plegando
pliego
pliega

poner — to put (down)
poniendo
pongo
pone

precipitarse* — to rush
precipitando
me precipito
se precipita

preguntar — to ask
preguntando
pregunto
pregunta

presionar — to press
presionando
presiono
presiona

probar — to taste, to try (on)
probando
pruebo
prueba

prometer — to promise
prometiendo
prometo
promete

quedarse* — to stay
quedando
me quedo
se queda

quemar — to burn
quemando
quemo
quema

querer — to want, to love
queriendo
quiero
quiere

recoger — to pick (flowers)
recogiendo
recojo
recoge

recortar — to cut out
recortando
recorto
recorta

regalar — to give (a gift)
regalando
regalo
regala

reírse* — to laugh
riendo
me río
se ríe

remendar — to mend (clothes)
remendando
remiendo
remienda

resbalarse* — to slip
resbalando
me resbalo
se resbala

rescatar — to rescue
rescatando
rescato
rescata

respirar — to breathe
respirando
respiro
respira

revolver — to stir
revolviendo
revuelvo
revuelve

romper — to break
rompiendo
rompo
rompe

saber — to know (facts)
sabiendo
sé
sabe

sacudir — to shake
sacudiendo
sacudo
sacude

salpicar — to splash
salpicando
salpico
salpica

saltar — to jump
saltando
salto
salta

saludar (con la mano) — to wave
saludando
saludo
saluda

salvar — to save (from danger)
salvando
salvo
salva

secar — to dry
secando
seco
seca

señalar — to point
señalando
señalo
señala

sentarse* — to sit down
sentando
me siento
se sienta

sentirse* — to feel
sintiendo
me siento
se siente

significar — to mean
significando
significo
significa

sonar — to sound, to ring
sonando
sueno
suena

sonreír — to smile
sonriendo
sonrío
sonríe

soplar — to blow
soplando
soplo
sopla

sostener — to hold
sosteniendo
sostengo
sostiene

subir — to climb
subiendo
subo
sube

tener — to have
teniendo
tengo
tiene

terminar — to finish
terminando
termino
termina

tirar — to pull, to throw, to knock over
tirando
tiro
tira

tocar — to touch, to feel, to play (music)
tocando
toco
toca

trabajar — to work
trabajando
trabajo
trabaja

traer — to bring
trayendo
traigo
trae

tropezar — to bump
tropezando
tropiezo
tropieza

unir — to join
uniendo
uno
une

usar — to use
usando
uso
usa

vender — to sell
vendiendo
vendo
vende

venir — to come
viniendo
vengo
viene

ver — to see
viendo
veo
ve

vestirse* — to dress
vistiendo
me visto
se viste

visitar — to visit
visitando
visito
visita

vivir — to live
viviendo
vivo
vive

volar — to fly
volando
vuelo
vuela

*see Reflexive verbs on page 100.

a menos que	unless
a menudo	often
(correr) a toda prisa	to rush
a través	through, across
a veces	sometimes
la abeja	bee
abierto	open (shop)
abrazar	to hug
abrigado	warm (clothes)
el abrigo	coat
abril	April
abrir	to open
la abuela	grandmother
Abuela	Grandma
el abuelo	grandfather
Abuelo	Grandpa
los abuelos	grandparents
aburrido	dull, boring
acá	here
acampar	to camp
el aceite	oil
acordarse	to remember
acostarse	to lie down
el actor	actor
la actriz	actress
además	also
adiós	goodbye
adivinar	to guess
la adulta	adult (f)
el adulto	adult (m)
afilado	sharp
afuera	outside
agarrar	to catch
agosto	August
el agua (f)	water
el aguacero	shower (rain)
el águila (f)	eagle
la aguja	needle
el agujero	hole
ahora	now
ahorrar	to save (time or money)
el aire	air
al lado	beside
el álbum de fotos	photo album
alcanzar	to reach
el alfabeto	alphabet
la alfombra	rug
algo	something
alguien	somebody, someone
algún, alguna, algunos, algunas	any, some
allí	there
la almendra	almond
la almohada	pillow
alojarse	to stay (visit)
alrededor de	about, more or less
alto	high, tall
la altura	height
la alumna	pupil (f)
el alumno	pupil (m)
amable	kind, friendly
amarillo	yellow
la ambulancia	ambulance
la amiga	friend (f)
el amigo	friend (m)
ancho	wide
andar	to walk
el ángel	angel
el anillo	ring
el animal	animal
antes	before
añadir	to add
el año	year
apagado	dull (color)
apagar	to blow out
aprender	to learn
apurarse	to hurry
la araña	spider
el árbol	tree
el arbusto	bush
el arco iris	rainbow
la ardilla	squirrel
la arena	sand
arreglar	to fix, to mend
arrodillarse	to kneel down
el arroz	rice
el arte	art
el artista	artist (m)
la artista	artist (f)
la arveja	pea
asentir con la cabeza	to nod
así	so (because of this)
el asiento	seat
la aspiradora	vacuum cleaner
el astronauta	astronaut (m)
la astronauta	astronaut (f)
atar	to tie
el aula (f)	classroom
el autobús	bus
la avellana	hazelnut
el avión	plane
ayer	yesterday
ayudar	to help
el azúcar	sugar
azul	blue
el babero	bib
la babosa	slug
bailar	to dance
la bailarina	ballerina
bajo	low
la ballena	whale
el banco	bank
la bandera	flag
la bañera	bathtub
el baño	restroom
barato	cheap
la barba	beard
la barbilla	chin
el barco	ship
la barra	bar
barrer	to sweep
el barro	mud
la base	base
bastante	fairly
el bate	(sports) bat
el bebé	baby
beber	to drink
besar	to kiss
un beso	x (kiss)
la bicicleta	bicycle
bien	well
blanco	white
la boca	mouth
el bol	bowl
el boleto	ticket
la bolsa	(plastic) bag
el bolsillo	pocket
el bolso	bag
el bombero	firefighter
bonito	nice (to look at), pretty
el borde	edge
el bosque	forest, wood
bostezar	to yawn
la bota	boot
el bote	boat
la botella	bottle
el botón	button
el brazo	arm
brillante	bright
la bruja	witch
bueno	good
la bufanda	scarf
el burro	donkey
buscar	to search
el caballero	knight
el caballo	horse
la cabeza	head
la cabra	goat
el cabrito	kid
el cacahuate	peanut
el cachorro	puppy
cada	each, every
caer	to fall
caerse	to fall over
el café	café, coffee
la caja	box
la calabaza	pumpkin
el calcetín	sock
calentar	to heat
cálido	warm
caliente	hot
la calle	street
calvo	bald
la cama	bed
la cámara	camera
la camarera	waitress
el camarero	waiter
el camello	camel
el camino	road, way
el camión	truck
la camisa	shirt
la camiseta	T-shirt
el campo	countryside, field
la canción	song
el canguro	kangaroo

Spanish word list

cantar	to sing	la cocina	kitchen	la cuchara	spoon
la cantidad	amount	cocinar	to cook	el cuchillo	knife
la cara	face	la cocinera	chef (f)	el cuello	neck
el caracol	snail	el cocinero	chef (m)	el cuento	story
la carne	meat	el cocodrilo	crocodile	la cuerda	rope, string
la carnicera	butcher (f)	el codo	elbow	el cuerpo	body
el carnicero	butcher (m)	el cohete	rocket	el cuestionario	quiz
caro	expensive	la cola	tail	la cueva	cave
la carrera	race	el colegio	school	(tener) cuidado	to watch
la carta	letter	colgar	to hang		(be careful)
la casa	home, house	la coliflor	cauliflower	la cumbre	peak (mountain)
la cáscara	shell (eggs, nuts), skin	la colina	hill	el cumpleaños	birthday
	(fruit, vegetable)	el collar	necklace	cuyo	whose
el casco	helmet	el color	color		
casi	almost	columpiarse	to swing	dar	to give
el castillo	castle	el columpio	swing	dar de comer	to feed
catorce	fourteen	comer	to eat	dar las gracias	to thank
cavar	to dig	la cometa	kite	dar saltos	to hop
el CD	CD	la comida	food, lunch, meal	darse cuenta	to notice
la cebolla	onion	como	like	de	of
la cebra	zebra	compartir	to share	de noche	dark (not daylight)
la cena	dinner	comprar	to buy	de quién	whose (in question)
el centro	center	la computadora	computer	debajo	below, under
el cepillo	brush, hairbrush	con	with	décimo	tenth
el cepillo de	toothbrush	con retraso	late (not on time)	decir	to say, to tell (give
dientes		la conchilla	(sea) shell		instructions)
cerca	close	conducir	to lead (direction)	el dedo	finger
los cereales	cereal	el conejo	rabbit	el dedo del pie	toe
la cereza	cherry	el congelador	freezer	dejar	to let, to leave
cero	zero	congelar	to freeze (something)		(something)
la cerradura	lock	conocer	to know (people)	dejar caer	to drop
cerrar	to close, to shut	conservar	to keep	del todo	quite, completely
el cesto	basket	construir	to build	delante	front
el champiñón	mushroom	contar	to tell, to explain	deletrear	to spell
el champú	shampoo	contento	glad	el delfín	dolphin
la chaqueta	jacket	contestar	to reply	delgado	thin (person,
el charco	puddle	copiar	to copy		animal)
el chícharo	pea	el corazón	heart	el dentífrico	toothpaste
la chica	girl	el cordero	lamb	el dentista	dentist (m)
chico	small	la corona	crown	la dentista	dentist (f)
el chico	boy	correcto	right (not wrong)	dentro	inside
el chiste	joke	el correo	e-mail	el deporte	sports
el chocolate	chocolate	electrónico		derecho	right (not left),
el cielo	sky	correr	to run		upright
cien	hundred	cortar	to cut	derramar	to spill
el ciervo	deer	la corteza	bark (wood)	desaparecer	to disappear
la cifra	number (figure)	corto	short	el desayuno	breakfast
cinco	five	la cosa	thing	descubrir	to spot
cincuenta	fifty	coser	to sew	desde	since
la cinta	ribbon	crecer	to grow	el deseo	wish
el cinturón	belt	creer	to think, to believe	el desierto	desert
el círculo	circle	la cremallera	zipper	deslizarse	to slide
la ciruela	plum	la cruz	cross	desnudarse	to undress
el cisne	swan	cruzar	to cross	desnudo	bare
la ciudad	town, city	el cuaderno	notebook	el desorden	mess
claro	pale, light	el cuadrado	square	despacio	slowly
la clase	(school) class, sort	el cuadro	picture	despertar	to wake (someone)
el clavo	nail (metal)	cuál	which (in question)	despertarse	to wake up
el cobayo	guinea pig	cuarenta	forty	después	after, next
el coche	car	la cuarta parte	quarter	detrás	behind
el coche de	fire engine	el cuarto	quarter	el día	day
bomberos		cuarto	fourth	dibujar	to draw
el coche de	police car	cuatro	four	el dibujo	drawing
policía		el cubo	bucket	el diccionario	dictionary

diciembre	December	el equipo	side, team	flotar	to float
diez	ten	equivocado	wrong	la foca	seal
diecinueve	nineteen	el error	mistake	el fondo	back (room, bus etc.), bottom (cup, sea)
dieciocho	eighteen	es, está	it's		
dieciséis	sixteen	el escritorio	desk	la forma	shape
diecisiete	seventeen	la escalera	ladder, stairs	el fósforo	match
el diente	tooth	escaparse	to escape	la fotografía	photo
diferente	different	el escarabajo	beetle	la frambuesa	raspberry
difícil	difficult, hard	esconder	to hide (something)	la frase	sentence
el dinero	money	esconderse	to hide (yourself)	el fregadero	sink (kitchen)
el dinosaurio	dinosaur	escribir	to write	freír	to fry
la dirección	address	la escuela	school	la fresa	strawberry
divertido	fun	el espacio	space (room or stars)	fresco	fresh
divertirse	to enjoy yourself			frío	cold (not hot)
doce	twelve	la espalda	back (body), shoulder	la fruta	fruit
doler	to hurt			el fuego	fire
domingo	Sunday	especial	special	fuera	outside
dorado	golden	el espejo	mirror	fuera de	out of
dormido	asleep	esperar	to wait, to hope	fuerte	strong, loud
dormir	to sleep	las espinacas	spinach	funcionar	to work (function)
el dormitorio	bedroom	la esponja	sponge	el fútbol	soccer
dos	two	esquiar	to ski		
el dragón	dragon	esta noche	tonight	las gafas	glasses
la ducha	shower (for washing)	la estación	station, season	las gafas de sol	sunglasses
dulce	gentle, sweet (taste)	estacionar	to park	la gallina	hen
duro	hard (surface)	la estampilla	stamp	ganar	to win
		el estante	shelf	el gas	gas
echar	to throw	estar	to be	gastar	to spend (money)
la edad	age	estar acostado	to be lying down	gatear	to crawl
el edificio	building	estar de pie	to be standing	el gatito	kitten
él	he, him	estar de rodillas	to be kneeling	el gato	cat
el búho	owl	estar enfrente	to face	la gemela	twin (f)
el, ello	it	estar sentado	to be sitting	el gemelo	twin (m)
la electricidad	electricity	la estatura	height (of person)	la gente	people
el elefante	elephant	estrecho	narrow	el gigante	giant
elegir	to choose, to pick	la estrella	star	girar	to turn
ella	she, her, it	estrellarse	to crash	el girasol	sunflower
ellos, ellas	they, them	estudiar	to study	el globo	balloon
empapado	wet (soaking)	el estudio	study (room)	el gol	goal
empezar	to begin, to start	la excavadora	digger	golpear	to hit, to knock
empinado	steep	el excusado	toilet	gordo	fat
el empleo	job	explicar	to explain	la gorra	cap
empujar	to push	extrañar	to miss (person)	la gota	drop
en	in, into, on	el extremo	end (table, line)	gracioso	funny, sweet (cute)
en algún sitio	somewhere			gran, grande	big, great, large
en forma	fit (healthy)	fácil	easy	el granero	barn
en vez de	instead of	la falda	skirt	la granja	farm
encantar	to delight	la falta	mistake	el granjero	farmer
encima	on top	la familia	family	gratis	free (no cost)
encogerse	to shrink	el fantasma	ghost	graznar	to quack
encontrar	to find	fantástico	fantastic, great	gris	gray
encontrarse	to meet (by chance)	febrero	February	gritar	to shout
enero	January	la fecha	date	el grupo	group
la enfermera	nurse (f)	feliz	happy	el guante	glove
el enfermero	nurse (m)	feo	ugly	guardar	to keep
enfrente	opposite, facing	la fiesta	party	el guijarro	pebble
enojado	angry	fijar	to attach	la guitarra	guitar
enorme	enormous	el fin	end (story, time)	gustar	to please
la ensalada	salad	fingir	to pretend		
entender	to understand	fino	thin, fine	la habichuela	bean
entonces	then	firmar	to sign	la habitación	room (in house)
entorno a	around	la flauta	recorder	hablar	to speak, to talk
entre	between	la flor	flower	hacer	to do, to make, to cook
enviar	to send	el florero	vase		

Spanish word list

hacer juego	to match	ir	to go	liso	straight (hair)
hacer malabarismos	to juggle	ir a la cabeza	to lead (be in front)	la lista	list
		ir a pie	to go on foot	listo	ready
hacerse socio	to join (become a member)	ir de camping	to go camping	llamar	to call
		ir de puntillas	to creep	la llave	key
hacia abajo	down	ir en bicicleta	to cycle	llegar	to arrive, to come, to reach
el hada (f)	fairy	irse	to leave (a place)		
la hamburguesa	burger, hamburger	la isla	island	llenar	to fill
el hámster	hamster	izquierdo	left (not right)	lleno	full
la harina	flour			llevar	to carry, to take, to wear, to bring
hasta	until	el jabón	soap		
hay	there's	el jardín	garden	llevarse	to take (steal)
el hechizo	spell	el jardín zoológico	zoo	llorar	to cry
el hecho	fact			llover	to rain
la heladera	refrigerator	la jaula	cage	la lluvia	rain
el helado	ice cream	el jerbo	gerbil	lo que	what
helarse	to freeze	la jirafa	giraffe	el loro	parrot
el helicóptero	helicopter	joven	young	el lugar	place, room, space
la hermana	sister	el juego	game	la luna	moon
el hermano	brother	jueves	Thursday	lunes	Monday
hermoso	beautiful	jugar	to play	la luz	light
el hielo	ice	el jugo	juice		
la hierba	grass	el juguete	toy	la madera	wood
la hija	daughter	julio	July	la madre	mother
el hijo	son	la jungla	jungle	maduro	ripe
los hijos	children	junio	June	la maestra	teacher (f)
la hilera	line (of people)	junto	together	el maestro	teacher (m)
el hipopótamo	hippopotamus			la magia	magic
la hoja	leaf, sheet of paper	el labio	lip	la maleta	suitcase
hola	hello	al lado	next to, beside	malo	bad
el hombre	man	el lado	side, edge	Mamá	Mom
el hombre rana	diver	ladrar	to bark	la mañana	morning
el hombro	shoulder	el lago	lake	mañana	tomorrow
la hora	hour, o'clock, time (on a clock)	la laguna	pond	la mancha	spot
		lamer	to lick	manejar	to drive
la hormiga	ant	la lámpara	lamp	la manga	sleeve
hornear	to bake	el lápiz	pencil	el mango	handle (knife, pan)
el hospital	hospital	el lápiz de cera	crayon	el maní	peanut
el hot dog	hotdog	el largo	length	la mano	hand
el hotel	hotel	largo	long	manso	gentle (animal)
hoy	today	el lavabo	sink (bathroom)	la manta	blanket
el hoyo	hole (in ground)	la lavadora	washing machine	mantenerse en equilibrio	to balance
el hueso	bone	lavar	to wash		
el huevo	egg	lavarse	to wash yourself	la mantequilla	butter
hundirse	to sink	le	her, him, you	la manzana	apple
		la lección	lesson	el mapa	map
la idea	idea	la leche	milk	la máquina	machine
el idioma	(foreign) language	la lechuga	lettuce	el mar	sea
igual	equal	leer	to read	el marinero	sailor
impar	odd (number)	lejos	far	la marioneta	puppet
importar	to matter	la lengua	tongue	la mariposa	butterfly
el incendio	fire (house on fire)	el lenguaje	language	la mariposa nocturna	moth
inclinarse	to lean	lento	slow		
infeliz	unhappy	el león	lion	la mariquita	ladybug
inmóvil	still (not moving)	les	them	marrón	brown
el inodoro	toilet	levantar	to lift	martes	Tuesday
el insecto	insect, bug	levantarse	to stand up	el martillo	hammer
intentar	to try	libre	free (unrestricted)	marzo	March
Internet (m)	Internet	el libro	book	más	more
la inundación	flood	ligero	light (not heavy)	el más, la más los más, las más	most
el invierno	Winter	el limón	lemon		
la invitación	invitation	limpiar	to clean	la mascota	pet
la invitada	guest, visitor (f)	limpio	clean	matar	to kill
el invitado	guest, visitor (m)	la línea	line (on paper)	mayo	May
invitar	to invite				

(la persona) mayor	grown-up	(de color) naranja	orange (color)	otra vez	again
la media	half	la nariz	nose	otro, otra	other, another
la medialuna	crescent (shape)	la naturaleza	nature	el óvalo	oval
la médica	doctor (f)	la nave espacial	spacecraft	la oveja	sheep
la medicina	medicine	Navidad (f)	Xmas, Christmas		
el médico	doctor (m)	necesitar	to need	el padre	father
el medio	half, middle	negro	black	los padres	parents
medir	to measure	nevar	to snow	pagar	to pay
el melocotón	peach	la nevera	refrigerator	la página	page
menos	less	ni un, ni una	no (not one)	el país	country, nation
el mensaje	message	el nido	nest	el pájaro	bird
mentir	to lie (not tell truth)	los nietos	grandchildren	la palabra	word
el mercado	market	la nieve	snow	el palacio	palace
el mes	month	la niña	child, girl	la paleta	sports bat
la mesa	table	el niño	child	pálido	light (color), pale
el metal	metal	el niño pequeño	toddler	el palo	stick
meter	to put (inside)	no	no (not yes), not	el pan	bread
mezclar	to mix	la noche	night	el pan tostado	toast
mí	me	el nombre	name	el panadero	baker (m)
mí mismo	myself	normalmente	usually	la panadera	baker (f)
mi, mis	my	nos	us	el pantalón corto	shorts
el microondas	microwave	nosotros	we, us		
la miel	honey	la nota	note (message, music)	la papa	potato
mientras	while			Papá	Dad
miércoles	Wednesday	las noticias	news	el papel	paper
mil	thousand	noveno	ninth	par	even
minúsculo	tiny	noventa	ninety	el par	pair
el minuto	minute	noviembre	November	para	for
mirar	to look, to watch	la nube	cloud	el paracaídas	parachute
mismo	same	el nudo	knot	el paraguas	umbrella
la mitad	half (portion)	nuestro, nuestra, nuestros, nuestras	our	parar	to stop (someone or something)
el modelo	model				
el modelo a escala	(scale) model	nueve	nine	pararse	to stop (yourself)
		nuevo	new	la pared	wall (of room)
el modo	way, method	la nuez	walnut	el parque	park
mojado	wet	el número	number	la parte	part
molestar	to bother, to disturb	nunca	never	la parte de atrás	back (from outside)
molesto	upset			la parte superior	top
la moneda	coin	o	or	el partido	game
el mono	ape, monkey	la oca	goose	la pasa	raisin
el monopatín	scooter	el océano	ocean	el pasado	past (history)
la montaña	mountain	ochenta	eighty	pasar	to happen, to pass, to spend (time)
montar (a caballo)	to ride (a horse)	ocho	eight		
morado	purple	octavo	eighth	la pasta de dientes	toothpaste
morder	to bite	octubre	October		
morirse	to die	ocupado	busy	el pastel	cake, cupcake
la mosca	fly	odiar	to hate	patear	to kick
mostrar	to show	oír	to hear	patinar	to skate
la moto	motorcycle, scooter (with motor)	el ojo	eye	el patio de recreo	playground (school)
		la ola	wave		
mover	to move	oler	to smell	el patito	duckling
mucho, mucha, muchos, muchas	(a) lot, much, many	olvidar	to forget	el pato	duck
		once	eleven	el pavo	turkey
la mujer	woman	opuesto	opposite (different)	el payaso	clown
el mundo	world	la orca	killer whale	el pedazo	piece
la muñeca	doll	la oreja	ear	pedir	to ask (for something)
el murciélago	bat (animal)	el oro	gold		
el muro	wall	la orquesta	band, orchestra	el pegamento	glue
la música	music	la oruga	caterpillar	pegar	to stick, to glue
muy	very	os	you	el peine	comb
		oscuro	dark (color)	pelearse	to fight
nadar	to swim	el osito	teddy bear	peligroso	dangerous
la naranja	orange (fruit)	el oso	bear	el pelo	fur, hair
		el otoño	Fall	la pelota	ball

Spanish word list

pensar	to think, to consider	la porción	slice (cake)	la red	net (for fishing)
el pepino	cucumber	porque	because	la Red	Net (Internet)
pequeño	small, young	el potro	foal	redondo	round
la pera	pear	el precio	price	regalar	to give (as gift)
perder	to lose, to miss (train, ball)	precipitarse	to rush	el regalo	gift, present
		la pregunta	question	la regla	ruler
perezoso	lazy	preguntar	to ask (question)	la reina	queen
el periódico	newspaper	el premio	prize	reírse	to laugh
pero	but	presionar	to press	el reloj	clock
el perro	dog	la prima	cousin (f)	el reloj (de pulsera)	watch
perseguir	to chase	el primo	cousin (m)		
la persona	person	la primavera	Spring	remendar	to mend (clothes)
pertenecer	to belong	primero	first	la remolacha	beetroot
pesado	heavy	la princesa	princess	de repente	suddenly
pescar	to fish	principal	main	resbalarse	to slip
el pez	fish	el príncipe	prince	rescatar	to rescue
el piano	piano	probar	to taste, to try	el resfrío	cold (illness)
el picaporte	door handle	probarse	to try, to try on	respirar	to breathe
picar	to itch, to sting	el profesor	teacher (m)	la respuesta	answer
el picnic	picnic	la profesora	teacher (f)	al revés	upside down
el pico	beak	profundo	deep	revolver	to stir
el pie	foot (body), bottom (stairs, hill)	prometer	to promise	el rey	king
		pronto	soon	rico	rich
la piedra	stone	propio	own	el rinoceronte	rhinoceros, rhino
la piel	fur (on clothes), skin	próximo	next (following)	el río	river
la pierna	leg	el puente	bridge	riquísimo	delicious
la pieza	piece	la puerta	door, gate	el robot	robot
el piloto	pilot (m)	el pulgar	thumb	la roca	rock (stone)
la piloto	pilot (f)	el pulpo	octopus	el rock	rock (music)
la pimienta	pepper (spice)	pum	bang	la rodaja	slice (meat, cheese)
el pimiento	pepper (vegetable)	la punta	point, tip	la rodilla	knee
la piña	pineapple	el punto	point (score)	rojo	red
el pingüino	penguin			el rompecabezas	puzzle, jigsaw puzzle
pintar	to paint	que	than, which	romper	to break
la pintura	paint	qué	what (in question)	la ropa	clothes
la piscina	swimming pool	quedar	to meet (by arrangement)	la rosa	rose
la pizza	pizza			rosa	pink
la plancha	iron	quedar bien	to fit (clothes)	la rueda	wheel
planear	to plan	quedarse	to stay	el ruido	noise, sound
el planeta	planet	quemar	to burn	ruidoso	noisy
plano	flat, smooth, level	querer	to love (people), to want		
el plano	plan			sábado	Saturday
la planta	plant	querer decir	to mean	la sábana	sheet (on bed)
el plátano	banana	querido	dear (in letters)	saber	to know (facts)
el platito	saucer	el queso	cheese	sacudir	to shake
el plato	plate	quieto	still (calm)	la sal	salt
la playa	beach	quince	fifteen	el salame	salami
plegar	to fold	quinto	fifth	la salchicha	sausage
la pluma	pen			salpicar	to splash
pobre	poor	la radio	radio	saltar	to jump
poco	few	la radiografía	x-ray photo	saludar	to wave (hand)
poco profundo	shallow	la rama	branch	salvaje	wild
podrido	bad (food)	la ramita	stick (twig)	salvar	to save (from danger)
el poema	poem	la rana	frog		
la policía	police	rápido	fast, quick	la sandalia	sandal
el pollito	chick	raro	strange, odd, funny	el sándwich	sandwich
el pollo	chicken	la rata	rat	secar	to dry
el pomelo	grapefruit	el ratón	mouse	secarse	to dry yourself
poner	to put (down)	los rayos x	x-ray	seco	dry
el poney	pony	recoger	to pick (flowers, fruit)	el secreto	secret
por	through, (done) by			segundo	second
por delante	past	recortar	to cut out	seguro	safe, sure
por favor	please	el rectángulo	rectangle	seis	six
por todas partes	everywhere	recto	straight (line)	la semana	week

Spanish	English	Spanish	English	Spanish	English
la señal	(road) sign	el taxi	taxi	tú	you
señalar	to point	la taza	cup	tu, tus	your
el sendero	path	te	you		
la señora	lady	el té	tea	último	last
sentarse	to sit (down)	el tejado	roof	una	a, one
sentirse	to feel (emotion)	la telaraña	web (spider's)	una vez	once
septiembre	September	la tele	TV	unir	to join, to attach
séptimo	seventh	el teléfono	telephone	uno	a, one
ser	to be	la televisión	television	la uña	fingernail
la serpiente	snake	la tempestad	storm	usar	to use
el serrucho	saw	templado	warm (liquid)	usted	you
sesenta	sixty	temprano	early	ustedes	you (plural)
setenta	seventy	el tenedor	fork	útil	useful
sexto	sixth	tener	to have	la uva	grape
si	if	tener hambre	to be hungry		
sí	yes	tener miedo	to be afraid	la vaca	cow
siempre	always	tener que	to need (to do something)	vacío	empty
siete	seven			valiente	brave
significar	to mean	tener sed	to be thirsty	la valla	fence
silencioso	quiet (silent)	tercero	third	los vaqueros	jeans
la silla	chair, seat	terminado	over (finished)	el vaso	drinking glass
la silla (de montar)	saddle	terminar	to finish	la vecina	neighbor (f)
		el ternero	calf	el vecino	neighbor (m)
la silla alta	highchair	la tía	aunt	veinte	twenty
el símbolo	sign (symbol)	el tiburón	shark	la vela	candle
simpático	friendly, nice	el tiempo	time (taken), weather	vender	to sell
el sobre	envelope			venir	to come
sobre	over (above), about (story)	la tienda	store, tent	la ventana	window
		la tierra	Earth, land, soil	ver	to see
el sofá	sofa	el tigre	tiger	el verano	Summer
el sol	sun	las tijeras	scissors	de verdad	real
solamente	only	el tío	uncle	verdadero	real, true
el soldado	soldier	el timbre	stamp	verde	green
sólido	strong, solid	el tipo	sort, type	la verdura	vegetable
solo	alone	tirar	to knock over, to pull, to throw	el vestido	dress
sólo	just, only			vestirse	to dress
la sombra	shadow	tirarse al agua	to dive	el viaje	journey
el sombrero	hat	el títere	puppet	la vida	life
sonar	to ring	la tiza	chalk	el vidrio	glass (material)
sonreír	to smile	la toalla	towel	viejo	old
la sopa	soup	el tobillo	ankle	el viento	wind
soplar	to blow	el tobogán	slide	viernes	Friday
la sorpresa	surprise	tocar	to touch, to feel, to play (music)	la visera	peak (cap)
sostener	to hold			visitar	to visit
su, sus	his, her, its, their, your	todavía	still, yet	la vista	view
		todo	everything	vivir	to live
suave	soft, quiet, smooth	todo el mundo	everybody, everyone	volar	to fly
subir	to climb			la voz	voice
sucio	dirty	el tomate	tomato		
el suelo	floor, ground	trabajar	to work (do a job)	el Web	(World Wide) Web
el sueño	dream	el tractor	tractor		
la suma	sum	traer	to bring	el xilófono	xylophone
el supermercado	supermarket	el traje de baño	swimsuit		
		el trasero	bottom (body)	y	and
el taburete	stool	travieso	naughty	yo	I
la talla	size	trece	thirteen	yo mismo	myself
también	too	treinta	thirty		
el tambor	drum	el tren	train	la zanahoria	carrot
tan	so (so big)	tres	three	la zapatilla	slipper
la tapa	lid	el triángulo	triangle	el zapato	shoe
la tarde	afternoon, evening	triste	sad	la zarpa	paw
tarde	late (near the end)	el trofeo	prize, trophy	la zona de recreo	playground (park)
la tarjeta	card	el tronco	log		
el tarro	jar	tropezar	to bump	el zorro	fox

Hear the words on the Internet

If you can use the Internet and your computer can play sounds, you can listen to all the Spanish words in this dictionary, read by a Spanish-speaking person.

Go to the Usborne Quicklinks Web site at **www.usborne-quicklinks.com** Type in the keywords **spanish picture dictionary** and follow the simple instructions. Try listening to the words or phrases and then saying them yourself. This will help you learn to speak Spanish easily and well.

Always follow the safety rules on the right when you are using the Internet.

What you need

To play the Spanish words, your computer may need a small program called an audio player, such as

RealPlayer® or Windows® Media Player. These programs are free, and if you don't already have one, you can download a copy from **www.usborne-quicklinks.com**

Internet safety rules

- Ask your parent's, guardian's or teacher's permission before you connect to the Internet.
- When you are on the Internet, never tell anyone your full name, address or telephone number, and ask an adult before you give your e-mail address.
- If a Web site asks you to log in or register by typing your name or e-mail address, ask an adult's permission first.
- If you receive an e-mail from someone you don't know, tell an adult and do not reply to the e-mail.

Notes for parents or guardians

The Picture Dictionary area of the Usborne Quicklinks Web site contains no links to external Web sites. However, other areas of Usborne Quicklinks do contain links to Web sites that do not belong to Usborne Publishing. The links are regularly reviewed and updated, but Usborne Publishing is not responsible, and does not accept liability, for the content or availability of any Web site other than its own, or for any exposure to harmful,

offensive or inaccurate material which may appear on the Web.

We recommend that children are supervised while on the Internet, that they do not use Internet Chat Rooms and that you use Internet filtering software to block unsuitable material. Please ensure that your children follow the safety guidelines above. For more information, see the "Net Help" area on the Usborne Quicklinks Web site at **www.usborne-quicklinks.com**

RealPlayer® is a trademark of RealNetworks, Inc., registered in the US and other countries.
Windows® is a trademark of Microsoft Corporation, registered in the US and other countries.

With thanks to Staedtler for providing the Fimo® material for models.
Bruder® toys supplied by Euro Toys and Models Ltd.
Additional models by Les Pickstock, Barry Jones, Stef Lumley, Karen Krige and Stefan Barnett
Americanization editor: Carrie Seay

First published in 2002 by Usborne Publishing Ltd, 83-85 Saffron Hill, London EC1N 8RT, England. www.usborne.com
Copyright © 2002 Usborne Publishing Ltd. First published in America in 2003.